"It wouldn't do, you know."

"What wouldn't do?" she pursued.

"You, staying on here . . . I would forget myself . . ." he answered in a low soft note.

"Would you? I would like that," she answered quietly, her grey eyes looking full into his blue.

There was no resisting the impulse. He bent and brushed her lips gently with his own. Sparks of sensation shot through him, and he was caught up in sudden, overwhelming desire. Even as she pressed herself to him, gave herself to his kiss, he was pushing her away, saying all too harshly, "Go back to the house, Bee."

She ignored the roughness of his tone and snuggled into his arms. "But, my lord . . . "

"Go on!" It was nearly a shout. "Now."

LADY BARBARA

Claudette Williams

FAWCETT CREST • NEW YORK

A Fawcett Crest Book
Published by Ballantine Books
Copyright © 1989 by Claudette Williams

Library of Congress Catalog Card Number: 88-92204

ISBN 0-449-21280-7

Manufactured in the United States of America

First Edition: April 1989

*Dedicated to Donna for the ribbon
at Rombout and the Blue at Smithtown!*

Chapter One

Bee took her fence, nearly lost her top hat, straightened it on her head of tawny hair, and looked ahead for her partner's quickly vanishing form. She smiled to herself and shouted into the wind, "Donna, you wretch! Slow down!"

Donna heard her friend at her back and pulled on her reins. Nothing. Beau wanted to run. That was what she had asked him to do, and now that he was into it and enjoying himself, he meant to keep it up. Donna turned and saw that Bee was catching up, and she grinned at her.

Bee laughed out loud. "Look where you're going, child!"

"Child? I will have you know that a married lady has a superior place. . . ." She stuck out her tongue. "Child, indeed!"

Bee laughed. "At sixteen you are a child . . . a child bride and an absolute madcap. I swear, we are going too fast!"

They took their next fence flying and laughed together over the feat. Bee caught up to her friend and again reiterated, "Donna, we must slow our pace . . . hounds would never run a fox so fast, honestly."

Donna drew her horse up and collected him for a

1

trot, smiling all the while. "Yes, but, Bee, I don't want to come in with a slow time ... after all the fuss the men made about letting us in this timber race."

"It isn't a timber race, you ninny. It is a hunter pace. We are supposed to calculate how fast hounds would track a hot scent over this plotted-out course. We are supposed to use our wits, and by all that is—"

"Bee, you are going to swear!" Donna teased. "I thought ladies were not supposed to swear."

"Shut up, child, and let's ride ... I can't take this walk!" Bee laughed and started her horse up again for the final leg of the course.

As they approached the last fence and the finish line, they could see the members of their local hunt gathered and shouting them on. It was a thrilling moment, and Bee felt suspended in time as she cooed to her mare and softly, gently, asked her for more. Her animal was tired; she could feel her straining as she galloped to her goal,

"Heart, Missy, you've got heart," she whispered as the mare took her easily over the last fence and followed Donna and Beau through the finish.

"That's my girls!" shouted an exuberant male voice as a man rushed forward to take Donna's reins.

Donna whooped with high glee in a most unlady-like manner and nearly dropped into her husband's arms. "Weren't we wonderful, my lord husband?"

"Robby ... Robby, what was our time?" Bee demanded of Donna's husband as she jumped off her horse and turned to find her father, the Earl of Saunders coming toward them, the smile wide across his attractive face.

"One hour and ten seconds, I think," Robby answered happily and kissed his wife's hand.

Donna looked up at her tall, handsome husband and sighed with pleasure. "That's good; isn't that good?"

"Good?" Bee returned sharply. "I think it is great . . . isn't it, Papa?" She turned to her father for confirmation.

He shook his head doubtfully in answer. "I don't know, love; there are a few who came in under an hour."

"No! That is impossible. Papa . . . you are joking?"

"Isn't bamming you, love," Robby put in gloomily. "Saw it posted myself."

It was at this juncture that Lady Barbara Saunders lost all physical connection with the little group surrounding her as she focused on the object that had caught her eye. He strode toward them purposefully, strong and self-assured. He seemed taller than most of the men roaming about the field . . . taller than most men she knew. His head of silver-streaked ginger waves was uncovered, and she noted with interest the intriguing manner in which it framed his handsome face. His face? Arresting, in his rugged good looks; another man would have called him a man's man, for he had that look. However, it was his deep blue eyes that suddenly made her mouth open. Faith, she thought to herself, who is he?

Robby broke the spell of the moment as he exclaimed excitedly, "John, you old dog! You made it, then," with which he went forward, hand extended, dropping the reins of his wife's horse to the ground.

Donna objected to his cavalier behavior with an exasperated sound, "Robby!" However, as Beau started to wonder off, she hurried to take up the

3

reins and keep him in order, saying under her breath, "Men."

"Yes, but such men," Bee mused out loud. "Donna, who is Robby's friend?" She had fallen in step beside Donna, for their horses still needed to be walked down.

Donna looked around and frowned over the problem. "I don't know precisely. Robby has been jabbering all week about this top sawyer friend of his who would be stopping by for a visit. This must be he."

"What is his name?" Bee pursued.

"Lord Connwood ... yes, Lord Connwood. Supposed to be something of a Corinthian ... pink of the ton, you know," Donna confided softly. "Looks the part," she added after giving his lordship a careful glance. "But don't ogle him; he is already taken."

Bee's shoulders drooped. "Taken? Is he married?"

"No, not married, but about to be, to Lady Sarah Grey, House of Grey. Title to title, money to money."

Bee wrinkled her nose. "A marriage of convenience?"

"Hmm, I suppose," Donna returned absently as Beau pulled her along in his efforts to consume as much grass as he was able before she put a stop to it.

"No," Bee said emphatically.

"No? What do you mean, no?" Donna looked around at her friend in some surprise.

"No, he mustn't marry someone out of convenience. An arranged marriage for such a man? It is unthinkable."

"Well, 'tis done. Can't be undone," Donna said,

ever practical. "They have just about posted the banns."

"But they haven't yet posted the banns?" Bee asked almost hopefully.

Donna narrowed her gaze and warned, "Bee, get that look off your face. What are you thinking, Bee?"

"Well, if they haven't made it public yet . . ."

"The only reason they haven't posted the banns yet is because Lady Sarah is in mourning for her mother's late sister. Another month and she will take off her mourning grays, and his lordship will enter the announcement of their betrothal in the papers, and that will be that. Banns *will* be posted. It is what they both want."

"I think it is what their families want." Bee suggested thoughtfully.

"Well, look at him," Donna demanded in some exasperation. "Does he look like anyone could force him to do something he didn't want? He must want it as well."

"Sometimes, Donna, we don't know what we want and are swayed into thinking we want something because everyone says it is a wonderful thing, and then . . . and then—"

"And then along comes a zany like you, bouncing in on the scene and getting everyone all confused, you odious girl." Donna laughed. "I warn you that Lord Connwood is my Robby's very dear friend, and Robby won't like it if you kick up a lark in Connwood's direction and leave him in a bind!"

"Donna, if I kick up a lark, it will be to set everything to rights," Lady Bee retorted, her hands on her hips.

"How, my darling friend, do you know they are not already in the right of it?"

"I don't. It is something we shall have to decide."

"Oh, no, you are not drawing me into this scrape. I am now a respectable married lady," Donna said, putting her chin into the air.

"Very well, I shall keep you safely out of it," Bee answered amicably.

Donna eyed her defiantly, "You have never left me safely out of anything, and don't try doing it now. What are you planning, Bee?"

"Well, now? To get introduced, of course." She drew her horse along and moved in his lordship's direction.

Donna eyed the heavens and took a long draft of fresh-scented air before smiling to herself; this would prove interesting. Everything her lifelong friend did always proved to be interesting!

Chapter Two

Introductions had been easy, since both Robby and Bee's father were in deep conversation with the newcomer. Bee stood to one side and watched as Lord Connwood charmed her father with his easy manners. His smile was engaging, and his voice magnetic, and she was somewhat startled when he directed a question her way,

"Speaking of hunting mares, you have got a sweet goer there, Lady Barbara. I watched your last fence, and although she was tired and blowing, she took it in a nice steady stride."

"Thank you" was all Bee was able to return. She felt a fool.

"Yes, but I don't think we were fast enough," Donna pouted. His lordship laughed. "Looked as though you were."

"Bee! Bee!" an excited male's voice called as a man came running toward the assembled group.

"Fleetie!" Bee cried, going forward to take his hands. "What, have they posted the winning time . . . what?" She knew that something was in the wind from the expression on his face.

"Aye! You and Donna are within seconds of the winning time. They are just calculating it now . . .

overheard them. Come on, let's get over to the hunt secretary's booth."

"And you ... what about your time?" Bee pursued.

"Blasted ugly cob of Jeff's lost a shoe, think we are five minutes too slow to be on the ticket."

By this time quite a crowd had gathered around the booth in question. Bee looked around and saw that her father's groom had taken both her horse and Donna's in hand and was presently grazing them. She tugged at Donna's arm. "Do you come?"

"Do I? What do you think?"

In some haste and with more bantering they made their way toward the assembled crowd, exchanging jests with their neighbors and fellow hunt subscribers along the way. Bee's father leaned toward her and whispered, "Have a notion you and Donna are near the mark."

"Do you, Papa? Why?" Bee was excited but still doubtful.

"Look at old Wendricks. He is looking at you, and I'll be damned if his eyes aren't twinkling. You're a favorite, have always been a favorite, and he looks pleased."

"Oh, Papa ... I do hope so, if only to show up that dratted pudding face, Sweeny. He is forever cutting in front of us and making a fuss about the fact that I am a female."

The hunt master put up his hand for silence, and it wasn't long afterward that he got it. Everyone waited expectantly as he smiled and began his speech. He thanked the wives of various members for setting up the hospitality booth with their cakes and tarts. He thanked the subscribers who helped lay out the course with their arrows and markers, and then he thanked all the participants for their enthusiasm, for they had certainly raised enough funds from the event, which would be donated to charity. As he spoke, he looked toward Bee, and his eyes twinkled,

"And now . . . I suppose it is time for the ribbons."

Some laughter and more jesting followed this announcement before he was able to proceed. There were ten ribbons being awarded to ten teams. He gave out first the "Turtle Award" for the slowest team; the two men were good sports, and while they hung their heads and took a great deal of backslapping, Donna and Bee looked at each other, for, again, the master had looked in their direction.

Eight ribbons were then awarded, and it was a good twenty minutes before the red ribbon for second place was held high and the master said, "It was very nearly a tie for first place, as first and second were only forty seconds apart, but second goes to Todd Michaels and Jeffrey Willards."

Donna and Bee looked at each other, and the smiles vanished from their faces. They hadn't taken a ribbon. Their time had been so close, by their own figuring, that they were sure they had taken a ribbon, but here they were, down to the last, and they couldn't have taken first. They were females.

The master looked at them fully now, and his grin was wide across his face. "And so, first place goes to two monkeys. They have hunted with us for a good number of years . . . nearly as soon as they were able to ride. They have taken their tumbles with the best of us, and they have hunted into the dark with us, never tiring. Their time was unbeaten today. Donna, Bee, come get your blue!"

It was some minutes later that Bee turned to find Lord Connwood's blue eyes on her, and she blushed. "I suppose I am making too much of a fuss. You must think me very silly."

"No, I think you refreshingly amusing," he answered her, with a smile that started in his eyes and lit his face. "And pink; you are very pink."

Oh, no, she thought to herself, he sees a child, only a child. She was spared the necessity of a reply, for Sir George Fleetwood came up behind her at that moment, picked her up bodily, and swung her around. "See that!" he exclaimed in high glee. "My girl takes it again." He set her down and gave her shoulders a squeeze. "Knew you would. As soon as the old man said that you and Donna would be allowed to race with the big boys, knew you two would take it. Stands to reason."

Bee laughed and made no objection to his handling. Theirs had been a longtime friendship. "Stands to reason? Whose reason?"

"Mine and anyone who has ever seen you hunt. Know how to get the best out of your animal. Now all you have to worry about is your animal's suspensory. It was pretty muddy going through some of that course."

Bee's face changed comically with her sudden concern. "What, did you see something I didn't? She didn't look off. I studied her, Fleetie, and she wasn't off, I'd swear. She wasn't even stiff."

"No? Well, I'd still poultice her tonight . . . just in case. Tell your man."

"It is a good idea," Lord Connwood put in softly.

Bee looked around at him. There was something, a superior commanding air about his presence. "Yes, of course, if you think so," she found herself answering.

Sir George put his hands on his hips in some indignation. "Aye, yes, if he thinks so . . . you little minx. What about me?"

"What about you?" Bee laughed.

"George, my boy," said Lady Bee's father, Lord

Saunders, as he came up to them, "we are getting up an impromptu dinner at the Grange tonight. Do you come?"

"Indeed, my lord, with pleasure." The tall youth smiled, turning his head slightly to pull a face at Lady Bee.

"Good," the earl returned, taking up his daughter's arm. "We'll see you then." He then turned to smile at Connwood. "I look forward to greeting you in our home later, my lord."

"Thank you," Connwood said, his eyes then moving to smile at Lady Bee. "Till then."

Lady Bee felt supercharged with electricity as she forced herself to look away from him. He was such a magnetically attractive man ... but he was nearly engaged to another. Drat. Double drat!

Chapter Three

Bee chose her gown with care, studied herself in the long looking glass, and frowned. She looked an angel in her pretty soft pink silk, but she knew enough to realize that she looked more schoolgirl than woman. The bodice of the gown was not low enough, and the cut not quite stylish enough. Her hair was thick and glowing in its tawny shades of gold, but she longed to put it up. That had been forbidden to her until she was formally presented in London. It wasn't fair, she decided; Donna was only sixteen and would have her hair up! Lord Connwood would never think of her as a woman.

Thus, it was that when Lady Bee descended the circular stairs to the central hall and smiled to see that the Huxleys had already arrived with Lord Connwood, she had no idea what an exquisite picture she presented. His lordship's blue eyes settled on her for a long moment and shone with appreciation. He then had his attention drawn away as his host put out his hand to lead them toward the library.

Lord Connwood lingered a moment as Bee gracefully managed the bottom step, and without effort and with much style, he took up her ungloved hand in greeting. He smiled and his blue eyes glittered

12

appreciatively at the blush that made its way to her cheeks. Softly he said, "You look ravishing, my Lady Barbara."

"Bee . . . I have grown quite used to my nickname over the years and prefer it . . . and thank you." She eyed him for a moment, considered him absolutely the most handsome buck she had ever seen, and said sincerely, "So do you!"

He nearly snorted with his amusement, but restrained himself so that he could gently kiss the fingers he still held. Her fresh scent came to him, and he looked into her gray eyes. "You are very generous. Ravishing, am I? And so I wish I could be . . . so long as my object were you."

She took away her hand. Here was a man like no other. His height towered over other men. His shoulders were broad, his body slim, his legs strong and athletic. His hair framed his face in windswept fashion. Even so, she rather understood his meaning and thought he had taken things a little too far.

He felt her withdrawal and smiled to himself. So, the child in her still was unused to mature flirting. He set himself to put her at ease once more,

"Bee, then." He inclined his head acquiescently. " 'Tis pretty enough, but Barbara is quite beautiful. I should dearly love to call you Barbara."

She wrinkled her nose. "No. You really must not."

He was surprised into asking, "No? Why is that?"

"Oh, you will think it silly." She sighed and avoided his eyes.

"Will I?"

"Yes. I am certain you already think me no more than a child," she stated sadly.

He laughed out loud and touched her elbow to stop her from going any further. His blue eyes twinkled at her. "No, how should I think such a thing?

I have been informed that you are nineteen and nearly an old maid."

"An old maid!" she snapped, her gray eyes flashing golden lights. "Who said such a thing?"

"As I recall, Mrs. Huxley," he answered promptly, "only this afternoon."

"Donna? Impossible. She is my dearest friend. She wouldn't, she . . ."

"Nay, nay, little one. She didn't put it quite that way. What she said was in answer to my question."

"Your question? About me?" Bee flushed furiously. "You asked her a question about me?"

"As we were due to have dinner in your father's home, your name very naturally came up."

"To what end? To call me an 'old maid'? That does not fadge!"

He laughed. "As it happened, I asked why it was that such a beauty as yourself had not yet been snapped up."

She peeped at him. "You are quizzing me."

"About what?" He was surprised. Was she unaware of her good looks?

"That you should think me a beauty after what you must be used to in London," she answered easily.

"My pretty Lady Bee, I assure you that I am certainly not just offering a piece of flattery. Now, why are you not married, or at least engaged? Donna tells me you have received offers enough."

"Oh, does she? Well then, why not ask Donna why I am not married."

"I did, and she said I must ask you," he returned glibly.

She laughed. "Well, I should think the answer rather obvious. I am not in love with anyone of my acquaintance. Don't want to marry for convenience . . ." She blushed as she realized she was touching a cord.

He didn't seem disturbed, however, but pursued the subject by asking, "And what of Fleetwood?" As he asked, he wondered why he did so.

She eyed him questioningly for a moment, but they had reached the library entrance, where everyone seemed to pounce on them at once.

Donna called her friend to order, indicating a sketch in the ladies' magazine she held open for inspection. "See, look at this, Bee. Do you think that pretty white print silk I bought last week would look well designed like this?"

"Too fussy," Bee returned, watching Connwood converse amiably with her father and Robby. Such shoulders he had! What a handsome profile. A smile curved her sweet lips as she watched his changing expressions; and then he was turning to wink at her. Hurriedly she looked away and reapplied herself to Donna's conversation.

The buzz of their liveliness was momentarily halted when the Saunders' small and elderly butler, Tuffet, announced the arrival of Sir George Fleetwood.

Sir George strode into the cozy scene with easy movements. He stood on no ceremony at the Grange. He went right up to Lady Bee, tweaked her nose, and dropped a kiss on her cheek,

"Hallo, pet, what are you at?"

"What do you think of this design?" Donna enlisted him at once.

He looked her tall, provocative body over and shook his head, "Too many fandangles."

"Ha!" Bee put in. "What did I tell you?"

"He's a man. What does he know?" Donna returned, turning the page.

Sir George didn't reply to this, for he didn't really listen to it. He was already moving toward Lord Saunders, who held out the lure of refreshment. Bee watched George thoughtfully as he fell into hearty discourse with the men. He was certainly a nice-looking man. Man? More a boy, especially when compared with Lord Connwood. She pursed her lips at this notion. It had nought to do with their respective ages, for Connwood would have the air of a man even if he were fourteen. There was an aura about him. Faith! What was she doing comparing the two? Fleetie was her dear friend, not a suitor, and Connwood didn't stand as either!

However, once more she looked at Lord Connwood. It was at this precise moment that he turned his head and found her eyes, and he smiled. She felt as though the heat in the room had suddenly increased.

"Bee! Ooh, Bee, come back." Donna attempted to recall her friend's attention.

"What? Oh, Donna, what?"

"What, indeed? You are daydreaming again, you silly girl. He is not for you. Get the notion out of your head. He will be leaving for London in a few days, and you will very likely never see him again."

"You are quite right," Bee returned in uncharacteristic meekness.

Donna eyed her doubtfully. "I am? Yes, you know, Bee, I am."

Lady Bee thought it wise to say nothing more on the subject . . . for the moment.

Chapter Four

It was early morning and Bee felt the tingle of the cool damp breeze on her cheeks as she ran her horse across the open field. There was still the tomboy in her, and it often landed her in some minor scrape or other. Perhaps it had something to do with being an only child, or the fact that she had lost her mother when she was still a babe, or the fact that she had grown up at her father's side and was as much a friend to him as she was a daughter. Never mind, she was comfortable riding astride in her faded blue velvet jacket and a set of tight old britches. The neighbors smiled tolerantly over such antics, for she was held in affection by them.

Lord Connwood held his horse in check and watched as she took her fence in fine form, stopped on the other side, and patted her horse. She was a pretty little thing, he thought to himself, and there was no harm in a mild flirtation. He put up his hand and he called her attention, "Ho there, Lady Bee!"

She looked around at the sound of his voice and felt herself blush. Faith, to be caught out in public by *him* dressed like a boy, and a raggy boy at that! If she could have, she would have hidden herself away. There was nothing for it now but to brazen it out. She smiled and waited for him to approach.

He seemed to take no notice of her style of dress but easily and with an air of amiable grace broke into light conversation. "Are you headed back to your Grange? I am myself going there to meet your father and your head groom—Chris Hubbard, is it?"

She was momentarily diverted into forgetting her state of disarray. "Are you? Whatever for?"

He laughed. "Your father did not tell you, then? Good, I like a man who keeps his women where they belong."

She put up her chin and glared. "And where, my lord, do you think they belong?"

"In a man's eyes, in a man's arms . . . and out of his business." He was smiling still, putting the lie to his words.

She grimaced at him, but there was a twinkle in her eyes, for she could see he was teasing her. "Ah, is that your way of telling me I should not have asked what you want with my father and Chris? Right, then. I am very sorry."

"I am only bamming, pet. I am coming to have a look at that black mare your father is so proud of. We are thinking of breeding her to my stallion, Bold Tim."

"Bold Tim? Bold Tim is your stallion? Why . . . I have seen him. I know him. Faith, I didn't know he was yours."

He smiled indulgently. "Aye, we stand our horses out of Searington Castle. It was my mother's . . . I inherited it some years ago."

"Searington? My word! Searington. Everyone must admire the foals that come from Searington Castle. Why, I never associated your name, your title, with Searington. How very exciting. Lady

18

Charm and your Bold Tim! Famous ... absolutely famous! What a combination. She is quite a mare, but she is a maiden, you know." She frowned worriedly over this.

"Hmm. So your father mentioned. Never mind. My people know what they are doing, and perhaps I may take care of this myself." This time he was looking her over provocatively, and there was no mistaking the gleam in his eyes.

He is a rogue, she told herself immediately. He flirts for the fun of flirting. There is nothing in it. Right. So, if one understands that, one may go right ahead and enjoy oneself, right? She gave him look for look and answered, "I should like that," and on that note she urged her mare forward and across the field.

He watched her for a moment, excited in spite of himself. She was nothing more than a chit of a girl, just a pretty little thing.

Lady Bee stood leaning against the railing of the brood mares' paddock and watched the mares grazing lazily in the sun's bright rays. She was daydreaming. Donna hadn't been by the Grange in days, but Donna was like that, and ordinarily Bee would not have given it a second thought, but these days were no longer ordinary. Bee had not seen Lord Connwood since that morning he had ridden over to see her father's mare. She thought of riding over to visit Donna at Huxley, but, oh, that would seem so obvious.

Obvious? She argued with herself. Donna is your friend. You can ride over there and visit ... You can, yes, but would you have done so ordinarily? No. Donna was in the habit of coming to Saunders. That was the way it was. Well, never mind. Her days had been busy enough. It wasn't that she was bored. Restless, certainly, but . . . ? She turned, for she heard the sound of a horse's hooves clicking against the stones and saw it was Beau at once, but the rider? Upon closer scrutiny she could see it was Donna, but Donna was not dressed in her usual fashion!

She stood and waited as Donna approached. "Well, look at you!" she said, and then added, "Dressed to the nines, are we?"

"Yes, don't I look like a diamond?" Donna laughed as she jumped off her horse and took up her reins.

"You *are* a diamond, you silly thing," Bee returned with a giggle. "Now, where have you been?"

"Ah, that is something you must guess at," her friend teased with a raised brow.

"Donna Huxley, *where* have you been?" Bee demanded in her threatening voice.

"To Searington, my child, to Searington."

"Wretch! Never say so, you odious girl."

"Well, I shall say so because Robby took me there yesterday. We . . . er, went with Connwood." There was a naughty look on her face.

"You went with his lordship?" Bee asked, her brightly amused smile leaving her face with ludicrous speed. "Did he . . . did he return with you?"

Donna sighed with mock regret. "No, he elected to remain at Searington."

The sparkle left Bee's clear eyes, and she pulled on a strand of her hair. Her voice, when it came, was a small one. "Oh, I see."

"No, you doltish girl, you don't see." Donna laughed, taking pity. "He stayed for a very good reason. Robby brought me back at an ungodly hour this morning because he has some business to manage here today, but his lordship took our promise to return by the late afternoon."

"Oh." Again the small voice.

Donna shook her petite friend's shoulders. "Stupid! We promised to return with you and your father."

"I . . . I don't understand." Bee frowned over this last. "With me . . . with my father?"

"Hmm, yes, of course. It seems your father had already made some sort of tentative agreement with Connwood to visit and have a look at that stud before he brings over his mare for breeding."

"He knows—I mean, Papa knows we are going today?"

"I think so."

"And I am to join him? Did his lordship . . . mention me, or was that your idea?" She eyed her friend doubtfully.

"I never said a word, though I had an opportunity to have a look at the lady he is about to become engaged to, and, Bee, it won't do."

Bee's volatile brows went up, and her eyes opened wide. "Why, why won't it do? Isn't she pretty? Nice?"

"Oh, yes, she is pretty enough, but she is something of a rattle. Chatters on and on, and something else I can't name, but more than that . . . Bee, they don't suit. They just don't. Trust me on this."

"Never mind that. I asked you if he asked for me as well as my father, or did you instigate that?"

"I told you, Bee, I never said a word about you. He did. Said I should make certain you joined our little party, as he rather thought I might like that."

"Oh," Bee said, her smile vanishing again, "he did it for you."

"Never mind why he did it. He did it."

"Yes, but, Donna, he is so far out of my reach."

"Of course he is, but you might as well enjoy a little flirtation before you take on your London season."

Bee smiled at that. "Indeed, for he is quite adept at that sport." Suddenly, in her spontaneous style, she flung her arms round her friend. "I adore you."

"Yes, you should," Donna said, disengaging herself and taking Bee's arm to lead her toward the house. "Now take me in for breakfast. I came straight here without eating, and I am famished."

"Yes, but we aren't going to make all day of it, for I want to run over to the parish and drop off a box of clothing for the fair." She eyed her friend. "We will take the gig."

"Hmm, yes, splendid, for I had a good look at the new minister when I was in town a few days ago. Have you seen him?"

"Mr. Craig. Yes, I have." Bee laughed.

"He is quite beautiful. I think we should take him some tarts when we go this afternoon."

"Devil, you *are* a tart!" Bee bantered, giving her friend a push. "I shall tell your Robby."

Donna shrugged. "Please do. Perhaps he may be roused enough to pay me a little court."

Bee laughed and pinched her friend's cheek. "Brat. You are a married lady and have already been courted."

"I want to be courted for the rest of my life. Oh, Bee, I don't want to be taken for granted and set aside like so many wives."

"Hmm," Bee agreed at once. "You're right, of course, but you know, some men . . . like Robby . . . well, they are more apt to rave about hunting than romance. That is just the way it is."

Donna grimaced. "So then, if I can't flirt with my husband, I shall do so elsewhere!"

Bee laughed and shook her head. There was nothing wrong there except the impatience and restlessness of youth. That would pass in time. Time? That was precisely what she needed herself.

Chapter Five

Searington Castle sat on nine acres of groomed and richly designed parkland. At its back, woodlands and green open fields stretched out for yet another fifty acres. Its tenant farmers were well established and prospered, and its history was deeprooted. Searington had stood since the twelfth century and was certainly of Saxon origin, though its present lord traced his heritage back to the time when the Normans had conquered and established the castle as their stronghold.

It was later, in the 1580s, that one of Connwood's ancestors modernized the castle, using the imagination of the Elizabethan era to make the place fit for hospitality. This particular ancestor not only adapted the great hall that was a major part of the original building but actually built an entire mansion flanking it. This was the portion of the castle that Lord Connwood loved and inhabited when he was in residence at Searington.

He stood now warming his outstretched hands by the huge fireplace that dominated the entrance hall. It was an attractive welcoming foyer, with large diamond lead-paned windows, beneath which reposed dark oak window seats. He had just come from the stables. All was in readiness for the antic-ipated arrival of his guests.

There was no real reason for the excitement he was experiencing, and he frowned over the matter. What the devil was working him these days? Never mind, he told himself, it was the Earl of Saunders's mare. Good blood there, and with his stud they should produce an exceptional foal. That was it. There, too, Robby was a good friend. As long as he was rusticating in the country, it would be pleasant to do so with his friends at hand. No more than that. . . .

"Goodness, John, have you just come from the stables?" It was a female's voice at his back.

Connwood turned and smiled as he went forward to greet the plump and pretty woman approaching him. "Sarah, what a very pleasant surprise." One day soon he would fulfill his and her parents' wishes by marrying the Lady Sarah. One day. He nearly sighed out loud, for he had always liked being a bachelor. It suited him, and though he found Sarah both lovely and likable, he wasn't yet ready to give up his single life. Again he told himself, never mind, for she was still in mourning, and nothing could be declared until that was at an end.

She got on tiptoe and lightly kissed his cheek, as he did hers, though her large bonnet added difficul-ties to the task. "Tinker tells me you are expecting your guests at any moment. Have you time to go up and wash away the stench of your horses, for I swear, darling, your clothing reeks of . . ."

He cut her off by patting the gloved hand he was slipping through his bent arm. "My guests are as horse crazy as I, Sarah. They shan't notice. Besides, as soon as they arrive, I will be taking them to see Bold Tim, you know, and then we shall all reek of

25

horses." He was leading her to the library, but she stopped him with a laugh.

"Yes, yes. Well, I hope it shan't always be so—horses, hounds, and hunting. There are other things." She smiled coyly at him.

"Are there?" His voice lowered seductively. "Come, we will go into the library, and while we are waiting for some tea, you will tell me what those other things might be."

She trilled a laugh and gently slapped his hand. "Naughty boy; but, no, Mama is waiting in the carriage for me. We are off for 'Spencers' for a few days." She eyed him. "Shall you miss me?"

"Of course, my sweet," he answered gallantly.

"Come then, walk me to the carriage and say hello and good-bye to Mama."

"Of course," he answered at once.

He found himself watching Sarah's departing vehicle and it was some minutes before he was able to turn toward his front doors; however, he was halted at the top step by the sound of laughter. He looked down the drive to see a lively party of riders and a coach. He smiled to himself, for from what he could see, no one was within the carriage.

Indeed, the Lady Bee, Donna, Robby, and the Earl of Saunders had chosen to take the journey on horseback, leaving the luggage to the boot of the earl's coach.

The girls were laughing at Robby's complaint, "But, Donna, I'm hungry. We can see the stud after we sit and take some luncheon."

"Oh, pooh, it will be dark by then, for 'tis nearly three now, and too late for lunch. We'll take tea after we have seen the stud with the earl and Bee. You won't wither away in the meantime, I promise you."

He sulked, and Bee laughed. "Oh, Donna, let the poor boy eat. We can have a look at Bold Tim later."

"Don't spoil him," Donna reproved in high glee.

"Nonsensical children." The earl laughed. "Look, there is Connwood."

His lordship was already descending the steps, his smile wide across his handsome face and his eyes set on Lady Bee. She looked lovely in her pale blue riding ensemble, with her matching top hat saucily tilted over one eye. Her curls were caught high at the back of her well-shaped head, though one long tress dangled over her ear. Damn, but she was attractive, he thought as he moved toward her father and put up his ungloved hand to clasp the earl's,

"Welcome," Connwood greeted.

"Your park is magnificent," the earl returned. "I am looking forward to visiting your stables.

"Never mind the stables," Robby complained. "I'm hungry, John, and this mad crew here say you won't feed me. You will, though, won't you?"

"Don't fret it, Rob. There is a buffet awaiting you in the dining room. Cook thought you might want more than the usual at tea."

"That's a good man," Robby approved happily.

The earl was dismounting, but Connwood had already moved to help Lady Bee from her saddle, and as he held her waist and lowered her to earth, he felt a certain thrill that kept his hands a second longer in place. "Lady Bee . . . enchanting as always," Connwood whispered softly.

She ignored this, though her eyes twinkled at him. "We made quite excellent time. Our driver and coach left a good hour before us, but we managed to catch him up and escort him here."

He flicked her nose. "I expect that of you, but not of your father."

She smiled at her father. "Oh, Papa likes a good run now and then."

"More then than now." The earl smiled fondly at his only child. "Bee has omitted telling you that we took a shortcut through the north woods. Saved us a good five miles, you know."

"Aye, but I took a good knock on the head for the effort," put in Robby, who had just lowered his wife to the ground, and he turned to grin ruefully.

"Did you suffer a fall?" Connwood was surprised.

"No. My darling held a branch for me but then that blasted Beau of hers took off and she couldn't maintain her hold on the branch. It whipped back at me, nearly sent me reeling."

Bee giggled, and Donna gave a short laugh before she linked her arm through her husband's. "Well, John, what first?" asked Donna directly.

Two of the livery boys had already taken the horses from the group, and Connwood turned after asking them to have the mounts walked before they were stalled and watered. "What first? Should we not feed Robby first? I don't want him to faint away."

Robby stuck in his plea immediately, and laughingly Bee took Connwood's offered arm and allowed him to lead them into the house. Quietly she advised him, "For my part I wouldn't mind a cup of tea. . . ."

"Certes, then, woman. Why didn't you say so?" He looked at her in some surprise.

"Thought I'd wait and see what everyone else preferred," she returned simply.

He eyed her for a long moment but said nothing to this. Robby was calling his attention at his back.

"John, they tell me Randall means to put up his gray against Trimble's big red."

Connwood turned, and as conversation became animated about the projected cock fight, Bee had leisure to study his lordship and sigh. Such a fine man . . . promised to another.

Chapter Six

"A zany!" pronounced the earl, speaking of his daughter. "You have always been a zany." He was chuckling and gazing at her fondly as he spoke.

Robby and Donna laughed appreciatively over the anecdote he had just recounted in proof of this, but Lady Bee took strong objection. She moved across the Oriental carpet in Lord Connwood's library, the pale pink velvet of her gown gliding gracefully as she gave her father's outstretched hand an amiable slap.

"Zany, indeed!" she said to him, her gray eyes alive.

Connwood had been watching her, and his lips curved. She was a provocative little thing with a most desirable body. He liked her mannerisms. He liked her laughter, for it was light; it was musical and spontaneous. If he wasn't careful, he might find himself seducing the chit. That he wouldn't do. He didn't play with virgin hearts. She turned, and her eyes twinkled at him as she reproved her father.

"Papa, what will his lordship think?"

"Precisely what he ought. That you are a dangerous little bird and he would do well to forget this projected outing of yours tomorrow morning."

"Oh, but, Papa, I have always wanted to visit Stonehenge and it is so very near," she pleaded.

"Well, as to that, it is not I that you should be pleading with, as I have some business in town that will occupy most of my morning. If you have your heart set on Stonehenge, it is poor Robby or Connwood that you should apply to," he returned happily, reaching for his after-dinner glass of port.

Robby scanned the ceiling and started to hum. His wife stroked his arm. "Robby . . . please?"

"Rocks," he said, looking at her in some puzzlement. "What do you want to go and look at rocks for? Have rocks all over the countryside."

"Not like these, Robby. These are tremendous and full of mystery," Bee put in, her tone enticing him to ask for an explanation.

He went for the bait. "Mystery? What sort of mystery?"

Connwood laughed. "First we'll go and have a look, shall we? Then we'll tell Robby about the mystery of Stonehenge." He moved closer to Bee and whispered in her ear, "You do that very well."

She felt a thrill tingle through her as she felt his breath against her ear, and it was with an effort that she turned halfway to meet his gaze. "Do . . . do what very well?"

"Intrigue, my little one, intrigue and captivate," he answered at once and then took up her arm. "Come with me." He didn't wait for her reply but turned immediately to her father and explained, "I am abducting your lovely daughter, for I want to show her another, er, zany very much like herself."

"I object!" Bee declared at once.

"To what, my girl? Going with me?" Connwood asked, twinkling at her.

She was blushing now quite furiously. "No, no

31

. . . but we have not established that I am a zany. Calling me so doesn't make me one."

"If it is your father who calls it, then I fear it must be so," Connwood said in mock grimness.

The earl laughed and waved them off. "Never mind, Bee my darling. A zany you are, but a delightful one at that."

Connwood led her out of the room, down the drafty hall, to a narrow corridor whose walls were covered with paintings of men and women Bee assumed to be his lordship's ancestors.

"Ah, here she is, Mary Margaret Searington. My mother's grandmother. I knew her for the first ten years of my life, and she was a joy."

"A joy that you call a zany?" Bee asked dryly.

He laughed. "Well, she was, and that was a part of her attractiveness. One never knew what Mary Margaret would be up to, and she was up to every rig in town. There is something in the way you laugh—in the way your eyes gleam—that reminds me of her."

"Absurd man, how can you say so? You were just a boy!" She shook her head. "You, my dear lord, are trifling with me."

He grinned at her. "No, certes, I am not. 'Tis truth, every word, I swear."

"Stop." She laughed to see him cross his heart. "Tell me, do, what things your Mary Margaret did to attain such a lasting reputation?"

"My dear, the list is long and outrageous," he started, but saw her shiver and frowned as he reached out and took hold of her shoulders, "Are you cold? Shall I take you back to the library?"

Bee shook her head of tawny curls, and her eyes answered him before her words. "Oh, no, please. Tell me instead at least one thing that she did."

She was like a child, he thought, for he could see

that she was cold, but she was enjoying herself, so he relented. "Right, then, one thing, and then it is back to the fire for you, my girl, for I don't want you coming down with a cold."

My God, he thought again as she clapped her hands happily in anticipation of the story. His expression softened for a moment, and he flicked her nose. "Brat . . . do you always insist on getting your way?"

Her happy expression vanished immediately and was almost ludicrously replaced by one of dismay. "Oh, my lord . . . no, not with you. If you would prefer not—I didn't mean to plague you."

He chuckled and nearly hugged her to him. "Ridiculous girl, you haven't plagued me. I was only teasing." He did, in fact, take up her hand and slide it through his arm as he led her back to the central hall, near the library, where a fire blazed in the huge grate. "Now, let me see, yes, I know. I shall tell you how Mary Margaret began her career as a Searington."

Bee giggled. "She married one. Your great-grandfather."

"Ah, but she was not supposed to marry my great-grandfather. Her sister Jenny was promised to the old gent."

"Oh . . . whatever do you mean?" Bee was surprised, "What happened?"

He smiled to see her fine brows drawn with puzzlement. "Mary Margaret had two sisters, one, Jenny, was a year older, and the other was five years younger. Jenny was promised to my great-grandfather. It was a thing arranged by both sets of parents, but Jenny didn't want the match, and neither did he. There wasn't anything either participant in the betrothal could do. Such was life.

33

They couldn't go against their parents' wishes, you see . . . not in those days."

"What did they do?" Bee urged him to proceed with the story.

"Mary Margaret took charge. She hatched a plot to save Jenny from my great-grandfather. You see, there was an additional complication."

"What complication?"

"Jenny was madly in love with the young minister, but he would not consent to an elopement, as such a thing broke with his principles."

"What then?"

"Mary Margaret went to my great-grandfather and asked if he would abduct the minister and Jenny and keep them overnight somewhere. To hush up the scandal, she reasoned, her parents and his would allow Jenny to marry the minister."

"Well?"

"I am coming to it." He glared at her and then tweaked her nose. "Things rarely go as planned. My great-grandfather thought the scheme ingenious. However, our young minister was made of stern stuff and escaped his bondage, for he had no idea he was being taken to his ladylove—and had he known, he might have tried to escape as well."

"Oh, no. Then what?"

"Jenny was a party to the scheme and was awaiting her hero on board my great-grandfather's yacht. He went there to send her home, but through some misunderstanding, Jenny thought he was there to run off with her and managed to hit him soundly over the head. Mary Margaret got news of our minister's escape and went rushing to the yacht, where she found her sister quite hysterical. She threw water in Jenny's face and sent her home. She was in the process of reviving my great-grandfather when she realized they were at sea. The crew had orders, you see, to set sail promptly at five o'clock, and that they did."

"Well, all she had to do was tell them to return."

"Not so easily done. Their orders were to sail for France. My great-grandfather had suffered something of a concussion and was fading in and out. By the time he had his wits about him, they were nearly at the French coastline."

"Oh, no," Bee groaned. "That did it."

"Indeed it did. He escorted her to Paris after they docked in France, as we have a bevy of relatives there, but the damage was done, and so my poor great-grandfather still had a bride on his hands."

"Well . . . but that is awful."

"Not really. By the time they arrived in Paris they were hopelessly in love with each other. Theirs was a solid marriage." He smiled over the memory.

"Oh, how lovely. What about Jenny?"

He laughed. "She married her minister."

"Good. I like happy endings." Bee sighed, satisfied.

"I hate to burst your bubble, my dear, but poor Jenny made life for herself, her minister, and Mary Margaret as miserable as she could, whenever she could."

"Well . . . but why?"

"I don't think her minister gave her what she thought she deserved in life, and there was Mary Margaret—wealthy, happy, taking the beau monde by storm." He shook his head. "Jenny found herself with too many children and not enough pleasures. She accused Mary Margaret of stealing my great-grandfather from her."

"Well, upon my word," Bee returned.

"Which ends in a moral somewhere if you want to look," he said on a mocking note.

"Oh, like what?" Bee pursued.

"Like one should always mind one's own business," he answered glibly.

"Wretch! How can you say so? If Mary Margaret had not helped, or tried to, she and your great-grandfather would not have made a match of it, and Jenny would still have been unhappy—and dreaming of a life that she never had with her minister. Seems to me that Jenny had a problem, but Mary Margaret was still in the right of it."

He looked at her a moment and again touched her nose. "Wise little puss, and again you remind me of Mary Margaret, for it was precisely what she concluded when she had told me her story."

"Hmm," returned Bee, satisfied, "tell me more."

He laughed and pulled her along the remainder of the way to the library. "Not today. Your father will wonder what I have done with you." He opened the library door and gently pushed her within.

She sighed to herself, for her time alone with him had been enchanting. He was everything that was exciting and wonderful. He was the man she had always dreamed of, he was the man that she wanted, and—oh, no—he was promised to another.

Chapter Seven

Bold Tim was a beauty! Connwood led him out, giving the chain over his nose a yank to keep the stud in order, as he was misbehaving on the lead line. The stud snorted in defiance, and Connwood called him to brook.

"Settle down, Tim . . . go on."

Tim arched his neck, and Bee stood back to better view him. He was big, a good seventeen hands, and his bay coat gleamed in the morning sun. He had one white stocking, and his tail was as black and silky as his mane. She cooed to him softly, saying his name, and noticed as he turned to the sound that his eye had a fresh wound just over it. "Oh, faith . . . what is that?"

Patty, the head groom, shook his head. "The crazy beast tried climbing out of his stall yesterday afternoon."

"For goodness' sake, why?"

"Lordy, miss, if we didn't have a time of it." Patty was still shaking his head. "One of the mares managed to get out of her stall while we was watering, you see, and out she prances to go and have a look at Tim. Well, no need to tell you what went on then. He bruised himself in the scramble, but nought to worrit about."

At this juncture Tim snorted and stamped his left foreleg furiously. His audience smiled at his spirit, and the earl moved closer, saying quietly, "One in a million, John. This lad is one in a million. We should produce a winner between us."

"Aye. Think I have one already. I have a colt, a three-year-old, racing at Newmarket tomorrow."

"Congratulations," the earl returned excitedly. "Who was the dam?"

"Crystal, from Grantham House."

"Oh, yes, of course. They produce some very fine horses over there—" But he stopped then and shook his head. "Nought to this stud of yours, though."

As if he had understood, Tim snorted with pleasure, and the assembled company laughed. Connwood led him to the stud paddock and turned him loose. Tim took two strides forward, shook his head in a show of strength, pawed the earth with his fores, went to his knees, and promptly and luxuriously rolled.

Connwood smiled and moved toward the earl to hold his shoulder and then take up his proffered hand. "Well met, then."

"Well met, John." The earl was much satisfied. "Now, if you young people will excuse me, I mean to take to horse and make my appointment in town."

They saw the earl off and were gathering their own horses for their projected expedition to Stonehenge when Connwood heard Bee's distressed voice.

"Oh, no, Missy, what have you done to your leg?"

Bee's mare walked out of her stall and a few feet onto the main flooring. It was obvious to the experienced eye that she had somehow pulled up lame.

The tone of Bee's voice had brought his lordship to her at once,

"Right front, I think," he said as Bee walked the

38

mare to him. His face was grave, his eyes thoughtful, as he quickly scanned the horse for any showy wound. He moved toward her and said softly, "Hold her still, love, and we'll see," with which he ran his hands up and down her leg, holding them for a bit over the fetlock area. He frowned and, without speaking, ran his hands over the left front leg and then shook his head.

"No heat . . . no swelling. Let's see about her shoulder." So saying, he palpitated the shoulder muscles, which caused the mare to flicker distressfully. "Aye, 'tis the shoulder, then." He patted the mare and turned to Bee. "Zounds, woman, it's a long way from her heart, so don't look like that. She'll do."

"Yes, but how . . . when could she have done that? I can't recall doing anything out of the ordinary on our ride here."

Donna had approached and had been silently standing by, her brows drawn in a frown. "Yes, but that last fence your papa said we shouldn't take . . . remember? Beau took it like it was six feet, and your Missy twisted over it. I was watching as you took it and saw her twist her rump in midair. I didn't say anything because she landed just fine, and it was a veritable nothing of a fence."

"Yes," Bee said, sighing heavily. "Papa said they wouldn't like it, and indeed Missy stood off it and then took it short." She turned sad eyes to Connwood. "It's my fault."

He reached for her and gave her a comforting arm. "No, it is not. Missy was schooled to take your command. She disobeyed by backing off the fence." He frowned. "Where, exactly, was this?"

"You know that last stretch of wood just before you hit the open wheat field?"

"Ah, yes, it cuts out a good two miles of winding

39

road. Indeed, I know that fence. Split rail, not high but odd in color."

"Yes, and the view of dark woods into bright field," Bee added, shaking her head. "Still, I didn't think she would find it a problem. Freak thing; she must have landed harder than I realized and twisted that shoulder. Papa and Robby didn't take that fence but found an opening a bit farther away and were smart about it. In fact, they took a more direct route to the road by doing that."

"Yes, I know that route very well, but never mind." He held Bee's shoulder still in his embrace as Robby came up,

"What is it? What? Missy lame, eh? What's to do?" Robby asked.

"Sh, Robby. Yes, Missy is lame," Donna answered.

"Aha!" Robby returned. "Told you not to take that last fence, but, no, the two of you have to *yahoo* it like a couple of hoyden schoolgirls everywhere you go."

"Do be quiet," Donna scolded him.

"Well, now we can't go to that place with the rocks"— Robby's eyes lit up—"so there is some good out of this."

Connwood laughed. "Sorry, my friend, but Stonehenge I promised the girls, and Stonehenge they shall get. I have a stableful of horses, and one or two that Lady Bee might be able to handle"—he eyed her mockingly—"if she promises to behave, that is."

Bee groaned. "Oh, now I suppose I have a reputation to live with?"

He laughed. "Indeed, my child, live it down. Be kind to Applejack, for I think he will be your mount for today. See if you like his paces." He turned and called to Patty, who was lingering nearby. "Patty,

have one of the lads saddle up Applejack for Lady
Bee, but as to Missy's shoulder . . ."

"No one else but meself shall see to m'lady's
mare. Don't ye worrit about it, my lord," Patty answered, taking the mare's lead and moving off with
her.

"Yes, but"—Bee frowned, going after Patty—
"she'll need a linament rub."

"So she will, and there is no better linament than
Patty's own concoction. Leave the mare to him, my
girl. She'll do." Connwood took her hand unconsciously as he led her onward, with Robby and
Donna following quietly at their heels.

Bee felt a thrill rush through her at his touch,
even through her kid gloves, but he was talking to
her and she centered on his words. "Here is Applejack. How do you like him?"

All the stalls at Searington were incredibly beautiful, with their highly polished mahogany panels
and their brass fittings. His lordship had opened
the wide door to Applejack's stall, and Bee was immediately nuzzled by a roan whose ancestry was
entirely questionable. He was not particularly
handsome, but then one would not say he was ugly;
however, he was in immediate contrast to his lux-
urious surroundings, and Bee giggled as she stroked
his velvety nose.

"He is adorable."

His lordship smiled. "Patty found him somewhere being abused, and it near broke his heart to
see it. Took it upon himself to rescue the beast, who
was nothing more than a colt then. We had him
gelded, and he has proved himself to be a faithful
mount."

"Aye, plucky thing, too!" added Patty, who had
come up at that moment from behind. "Gave yer

mare a little bute, m'lady. It will ease her distress, it will . . . mean to linament her now."

She smiled at him. "Thank you, Patty."

"Let's move off outside now, and my lads will see to our mounts," suggested his lordship, who saw from Patty's expression that this was the old retainer's wish.

Bee fell into step beside his lordship and gazed up at him with near worship in her gray eyes. "Thank you, my lord. You are too good."

He twinkled down at her, "Do you think so, my little one? That is because you are too green to know better."

"Do not say that," she returned at once.

He laughed. "Know me, child. I do what I want, for my own reasons. Always."

She eyed him a moment and then quietly, gently, and with a twinkle of her own, meekly returned, "Yes, my lord."

He looked at her sharply, laughed out loud, and flicked her nose.

"Brat!"

Chapter Eight

"Close your mouth, Robby," Donna said teasingly as she linked her arm through her husband's and turned to smile at Bee. "He is, as you can see, quite amazed."

"Yes, and he should be," said a grizzled man in a wool cap coming up behind them. He nodded and added, "I'm Mr. Harlan, and if you have any questions, I'd be happy to answer them for you."

"Yes, I do," Robby said at once. "I heard a woman . . . well, she said"—he lowered his voice—"those holes marked over there, that they were used as ritual pits."

"Aye," Mr. Harlan said, "she is quite right, you know. The whole place was used for rituals, or so our learned men tell us."

Bee and Connwood moved in closer, and Bee whispered to his lordship, "What does that mean?"

"Burial grounds. It is believed that the old religion used this perhaps as a mass burial ground," Connwood answered quietly.

"Aye, that's a theory. Aye, and not many know it or believe it, but it seems likely," Mr. Harlan said approvingly. "Look how those stones form a half circle. Think those poor devils lugged those stones all the way here over land and water just to

43

play at pagan games?" He shook his head. "They were Druids, they were. Three hundred miles—aye, three hundred miles from Western Wales, that's where those stones were brought from. Some say the Druids built themselves a temple here to worship the sun. But what about that earth wall you see there?" He pointed and waited for the effect of his words. "Well now, think maybe there was more to it than worship of the sun, making and marking of a calendar. Think important rituals went on here . . . burial rituals." He moved his head thoughtfully and then looked at Robby. "What say you, young man?"

"Me?" Robby nearly shrieked, so deeply engrossed had he become with the story. He shrugged his shoulders, lifted his hands, and dropped them. "This is getting too spooky by far. Let's get some lunch."

His friends chuckled amicably over the intensity with which he said this last. Connwood slipped the guide a coin and a thank-you for his efforts, and quietly they moved among some of the tourists studying the large blue stones.

"It's fascinating, you know," Bee remarked as she gazed at one stone in particular. "Imagine, with their crude tools they managed the feat of not only cutting out these exact shapes but then transporting them so many miles."

Connwood watched her eyes sparkle and smiled. "Awesome, when one considers it, though I think it is believed that at one time there was a waterway that ran through this valley, which would have made the project somewhat easier."

She eyed him wonderingly. "How do you know? Have you been here before?" She was finding his lordship knowledgeable in so many areas.

"Hmm, once before, as a boy," he said softly, "but

that trip is forgotten, and only this one will remain now in my memory."

"Your flattery is outrageous." She laughed.

"Not flattery, my pretty, I mean it," he said seriously.

She eyed him and gave him a rueful twinkle of a smile. "Oh, yes, but of course, my lord. Now ... come, Robby has been so good, we should go and feed him, and I am getting hungry myself."

"Good girl!" Robby approved, catching this last.

Bee and Donna stood chatting happily in the courtyard of the Red Lion Inn while the men spoke to the livery boys about their horses. Bee giggled over one of Donna's remarks and looked up to see Connwood smiling at her. Such blue eyes, she thought, as his gaze locked with hers. The next thing she knew, he was there beside her, taking her elbow and leading her within, Robby and Donna bantering behind them.

"Where shall we take a table?" his lordship said, more to himself than to Bee. "I think a private parlor, as the inn seems busy in the main gallery today."

The innkeeper came forward, and as his lordship discussed their needs with him, Bee found herself looking around the gallery. Her survey discovered a rather good-looking man with dark hair and a mustache leaning against the bar counter. He was well dressed; in fact, what had caught her eye was that he was very nearly overdressed for his locale. He looked to be more of a town beau, a dandy. As though he felt her scrutiny, he turned halfway, returned her look, and inclined his head.

Connwood chanced to look in the man's direction at this juncture and was startled to see the man in question had set Lady Bee to the blush. He felt somewhat irritated when he asked her, "Do you know that gentleman?"

"No, no," she answered quickly giving the gallery her back.

"Then perhaps I'll go and have a word with the man about the proprieties of looking where he should not!" Connwood said on a low, hard note.

Lady Bee's color went into the deepest shade of red possible as she extended her gloved hand to Connwood's hard arm and said, "Oh, please, my lord, do not . . . it would cause such a stir, and it was my fault."

"Your fault? How so?" he almost barked at her.

"If you will follow me, m'lord," the innkeeper said, "the private parlor is ready for you."

Robby took Donna in tow and moved off first. Connwood wanted his answer. "How so?" he repeated his question without taking one step away.

"I . . . I was looking about and I must have stared at him, you see. He caught me." Bee lowered her eyes to the floor, quite humiliated.

Connwood was annoyed, but at her confession, he almost laughed out loud. He could not help but think, as she studied the flooring, that she was like an adorable child, wilful and troublesome at times, but quite, quite innocent. "Aha," he answered and took her hand. "That is something perhaps we should discuss . . . later."

She looked up sharply at that and put up her chin. "I don't see that there is anything to discuss. After all, *you* are not my father!" She tried to pull out of his grasp, but he held tight and his brow went up,

"Oh-ho, my girl, and glad of it, but nevertheless, when you are in my charge, as you are for the day, I am afraid that you will adhere to my rules."

"Can't!" Bee returned naughtily and then burst

into a series of musical giggles. "Don't know what they are." So saying, she did manage to break from his hold and quickly preceded him into the parlor, where Donna and Robby were warming themselves near the fire.

Chapter Nine

"If you children will step aside, I will show you how this should be made," Connwood said, pulling a face at Robby and waving him away from the punch bowl.

"But it needs nutmeg," Robby complained, "and cinnamon. Tell Donna—"

"Nutmeg"—Donna wagged a finger at him—"will ruin it."

Bee wandered off from their lively dispute, took up a piece of buttered bread from the table, and moved toward the large window seat to look out at the cobbled rear courtyard. Something, the sound of voices perhaps, had caught her curiosity. Her brow went up, to see the innkeeper in a heated discussion with a brightly clad man. Further inspection revealed a Gypsy wagon painted in green, with yellow trim. Ordinarily she would have smiled with pleasure, but instinct kept her still and silent as she observed the innkeeper's movements. Something, perhaps a purse, was exchanged between the two, and the Gypsy, a small round man with a scarf round his neck and a wool cap pulled low over his forehead, grumbled bitterly as he moved toward his wagon. Bee watched him get up behind his team of horses and whip them forward. The wagon lurched, and for a fleeting moment she saw something—a child's fair face at the window within the wagon. Bee's eyes opened wide, for it was a little boy with large sad eyes. However, the wagon was soon out of her line of vision. Odd, she thought, but never mind, and she would then have turned to the bickering going on at her back over the punch had her attention not been caught once more, this time by the florid-looking dandy she had seen in the main gallery. He moved toward the innkeeper, and Bee fell back behind the hangings at the window, suddenly aware that she didn't want to be seen watching them. Again there was an exchange of purses, and this time the innkeeper was the one to receive the purse before the dandy moved toward the livery.

Connwood's hand on Bee's shoulder made her jump, and he laughed. "What is it, love?"

"In truth, I don't know . . . but I think this inn may not be what it seems," Bee said, her eyes wide.

"What do you mean?" Donna was quick to pick up on Bee's tone of voice.

"Well, I just saw the oddest thing," Bee said and then waved her hand in the air, "or perhaps I am just being silly."

"What did you see?" Connwood asked quietly, but he was observing her thoughtfully.

"There was a Gypsy . . . and he had his wagon just outside in the rear courtyard. . . ."

"A Gypsy? Here?" Robby asked immediately. "Famous! Maybe there is a carnival nearby."

Bee smiled absently over Robby's innocent enthusiasm, but his lordship took her chin and demanded, "What, Bee? What is it that makes you frown? Tell me, and I will set it straight."

"I am not frowning," she denied with a half smile, and gently withdrew.

"Tell me," he insisted softly. "Something has you bothered."

"Oh, I don't know. Perhaps it was that little boy. . . ."

"What little boy?" he asked in some surprise.

"The one at the window of the Gypsy wagon. He looked so very frightened."

"Aha!" Donna interjected suddenly. "Now, this is punch. Here, Bee, this will make you feel more the thing."

Bee laughed and took the glass being thrust at her. Connwood smiled and quietly said, "Such a sweet smile you have, my lady Bee. It must always be an object of mine to see that nothing interferes with your pleasure when you are with me."

"You are being outrageous again, my lord," Bee lively returned.

"No, I am not. I like to see you happy," he answered simply.

She almost believed him in that moment but said, "You are an accomplished flirt, and *that* is taking advantage of me, my lord, for I *am not*."

"I am not flirting in the least, but am most sincere. Do you believe me, my little one? Say that you believe me," his lordship returned, gazing tenderly into her eyes.

She twinkled at him, for his blue eyes were rich with amusement, and she gave his upper arm a gentle slap. "Cad! You do that so well, but I know better, even though I am nought but a poor green girl."

"Tell him!" Robby approved heartily. "That's right, run him through, put him to earth. It is just what he deserves."

"My friend?" Connwood returned, one eyebrow up as he looked quizzically at Robby.

Much jesting and rallying followed this, and the

Gypsy, his brightly painted wagon, and the face of the youth at the window were forgotten. The afternoon passed pleasurably as did the evening, and when the earl announced his intentions of leaving with his daughter in the morning, Connwood would hear none of it.

"Never say so, for Lady Bee's mare is not yet fit," Connwood argued reasonably.

The earl eyed him in some amusement. "A problem, but not one that I cannot overcome. I could hire—"

"Hire?" his lordship cut in on a note of horror. "So that is what you think of my hospitality? You would hire before you would take one of my own?"

"John," the earl reproved gently, "you are too good. I must return to the Grange in the morning, as I have some business to conduct with my bailiff."

"Leave your daughter, then, on the promise that you will return to us as soon as you may," Connwood cajoled, his smile as charming as his tone.

The earl looked to his daughter, who was trying to appear unconcerned with the proceedings. "What say you, Bee?"

"Well, I confess that I would much rather make the trip home on my own Missy when she is recovered." She looked to Donna. "You and Robby mean to stay on a bit, don't you?"

"Of course they are staying," Connwood answered for them and looked to the earl. "No harm shall come to your daughter while she is at Searington."

"Of that I never had any doubt," the earl returned promptly. "Well then, Bee, it is decided. I may not see you in the morning, as I shall be leaving early—" he moved to kiss his daughter—"but I will return for you within the next two days." He looked toward Connwood. "Don't let her run you ragged."

"Papa!" Bee objected.

Thus, the day ended on a jolly note, but still, just before Bee closed her eyes, a flash of remembrance of the urchin in the Gypsy wagon came to mind. Such a sad little face. It was her last thought before she drifted into confused dreams.

Chapter Ten

"I rather think he fancies you, Bee," Donna said slowly as she surveyed her friend for a reaction.

"Stop it," Bee answered, frowning.

"Stop it? Whatever do you mean, stop it? Just yesterday that was all you wanted."

"That was yesterday," Bee returned evasively.

"But—"

"Donna, I am not playing games . . . I am in earnest," Bee cut in quietly.

"I didn't say he was playing a game," Donna answered, and now she was frowning.

"No, you did not, but I rather think he is. His lordship is taken with me and amused perhaps . . . but he means to go through with his plans to marry his Lady Sarah and unite their family names. He believes in that sort of thing. I understood that last evening when he was talking to Papa about ancestors and family heritage."

Donna moved toward her petite friend and put a comforting arm about her shoulders. "Yes, I know."

"You will never guess!" Robby announced at the morning room's wide-open double doors. He appeared to be in high glee, "There is a carnival!"

Momentarily diverted, the girls in unison repeated, "A carnival?"

"Where?" Bee asked.

"Not more than five miles from here. Where is Connwood?"

"How do you know, Robby?" Donna moved toward him as he came into the room with his long, sturdy strides.

"Had it from Fleetwood," he answered happily.

"Fleetwood?" Bee asked in some surprise. "How could you have it from Fleetwood?"

"Why couldn't he have it from me?" Sir George Fleetwood asked as he entered the scene.

Bee skipped to him and held his lapels. "Fleetie! You are here, you silly boy. What are you doing here?"

"Well, what sort of a greeting is that?" he returned and slid his arm round her trim waist. "Thought you would be happy to see me, pet, and all you will call me is a silly boy."

She giggled and, still in his hold, got on tiptoe to plant an affectionate kiss on his fair cheek. "There! I *am* happy to see you, but that doesn't answer my question."

His lordship arrived at this moment and was surprised to find himself irritated to see the Lady Bee ensconced quite happily in Sir George's embrace. "Fleetwood," his lordship said jovially enough, "welcome. When did you arrive, and to what do we owe this pleasure?"

Sir George Fleetwood's friendship with Lady Bee was deep-rooted. His affection for her often made him wonder whether or not she was the lady of his dreams. However, before she had left for Searington, she had confessed to him that Connwood had caught her interest. He had frowned over the problem and warned her off. Lord Connwood was a Corinthian, a nonpareil, a top sawyer, and something of a rake. These things alone would have brought up a warning finger, but he also knew that his lord-ship would soon become engaged to the Lady Sarah. His little Bee was bound to be hurt. He rather thought he would step in and be there for her when she fell. He eyed Connwood and gave Bee another squeeze.

"To answer you, my lord, I have only just arrived. Been invited to put up with friends not far from Searington, but what really brings me to Searington is Bee. Missed her," he said simply.

Bee flushed and gently disengaged herself from his hold, suddenly aware of Connwood's hard eyes. She looked at Sir George and reproved him merrily. "Beast. You are not here to see me. How did you know I was still here and not on my way home with Papa?"

"Didn't," Fleetwood returned.

"Incorrigible." Bee laughed.

"Oh, by the by" Sir George said, directing this toward his host, "your stables are about the finest I have ever clapped eyes on. Good people you have there, too."

"Thank you," Connwood said, moving out of the way for the butler, who had appeared with a tray of coffee and biscuits.

"I say," Robby said, suddenly animated, "those hot buns look devilishly inviting." He moved into position, and Donna laughed and went to aid him.

"What about this carnival?" Bee asked.

"Yes, you would like that, Bee. Don't think we've been to a carnival in years and years," Fleetwood said, patting a place on the sofa.

She seated herself daintily beside him, served him the coffee Donna had poured, and sliced a hot iced bun for him as well. Connwood watched her and felt an irritation of nerves. She turned to his lordship and, her eyes bright, asked, "May I serve you, my lord?" She was already doing so.

He took the coffee from her and felt a thrill as her fingers brushed up against his hand. Absurd, he told himself. The feelings this child put him through were absolutely absurd, yet she was quite charming.

Bee found his eyes glittering, and though she had no notion what he was thinking, those shining eyes drew out her color, and she beamed at him before turning to fall into the conversation. Odd, Bee thought, his eyes had the power to trap her, claim her attention to the exclusion of all else. This would have to stop. She was a stupid, inexperienced girl, and she was behaving like a fool.

"Well, do we go, then?" Donna nibbled on a hard biscuit and waited expectantly.

"Of course," Robby answered at once. "There is bound to be a performing bear."

"And fortune tellers . . ." Bee mused out loud.

"Do you want to know the future?" Connwood asked her quietly, his eyes coming to rest on her lips.

She smiled at him. "Yes and no."

"Just like a woman." He laughed. "What do you mean, yes and no? Either you do or you don't."

"I want to know the good . . . not the bad," she replied cheerfully.

"Hmm," Donna agreed, "I wouldn't want to hear the bad that might happen to me in the future, not unless I could change it."

"Aw," Robby put in, "no one can tell the future."

"Robby is right," Fleetwood agreed. "That's just Gypsy games, but all in good fun. Let's have them put the horses—"

"No," Connwood said. "I think I will drive in my

open phaeton." He turned to Bee. "You would like that."

"Oh, yes," she agreed at once.

He laughed. "And if you are a good girl, I might let you take the reins."

"And what shall we go in?" Donna pouted.

"My open carriage. You can have my matched bays," his lordship conceded, "but only if you drive, Donna. Robby is too ham-handed for my bays."

"Done!" Donna laughed.

"Too ham-handed?" Robby grumbled. "I'm not too ham-handed. I can handle his bays. Tell him, Donna."

"No, darling. There are many things you can handle, but his lordship's bays are not among them." She tempered this with a kiss on his forehead and was already springing up. "Come then, Bee—we have to change."

Bee looked down at her pretty muslin gown of yellow. Her hair was done up with a matching ribbon, and she rather liked the effect. "I have a matching spencer that should be warm enough. Mayhap I'll stay in this." She was talking to Donna as she got up from the sofa, but it was his lordship who answered her quietly.

"Indeed . . . don't change a thing. You look quite charming just as you are."

She met his gaze and was momentarily mesmerized by his blue eyes. She felt like a silly schoolgirl, tongue-tied and awkward. "Thank you, my lord, but I will just go up with Donna and fetch my spencer."

"I will miss you until you return," he said softly.

Fleetwood watched this exchange and frowned. He waited for the girls to leave the room and turned to glare at Connwood. "She is a love, little Bee. The sweetest disposition. Wouldn't like to see her hurt."

Connwood would not have anyone dictate to him,

let alone this boy. His brow went up, and he said on a dry note, "Would think it very odd in you if you wished to see Lady Barbara hurt."

"Yes, right." Fleetwood continued to glare, but there wasn't much more he could say, especially with Robby happily munching biscuits. After all, it wasn't his place to do so; Bee had a father for protection, and as of now, Connwood had done nothing concrete to lead Bee on. How, then, would he save her?

Chapter Eleven

Bee looked fleetingly at his lordship's handsome profile and responded to his compliment that she was a skilled driver. "You are flattering me again, and it isn't at all necessary, my lord. You already have a place in my heart." She was being outrageous and knew it.

"Minx." He laughed. "You don't mean that."

"Which? That you needn't flatter me, or that you have a place in my heart?" she bantered.

"Both, you little wretch!"

"Uh-uh-uh," she cautioned with a giggle. "You are lapsing from flattery."

He reached out to touch her chin, but she put up a hand and warned him off. "My lord, I *am* driving."

"Are you? Then keep your hands on the reins, my girl, for you are coming to a sharp bend in the road and mustn't take it wide."

"Yes, my lord," she returned meekly, "if you will keep your hands to yourself." So saying, she broke down and giggled once more.

He looked at her happy profile and sighed contentedly. Adorable, he thought, the child is adorable. They were nearing the Gypsy campsite, and she was slowing down,

"My lord," she interrupted his thoughts, "take the reins. Do, please take the reins. Your grays are such steppers, and I am afraid I might do them some harm in tight quarters."

"Nonsense. Take them into the field . . . go on. You can do it, love," he urged.

She stopped the grays, though she did not brake the phaeton. "Thank you, my lord," she returned, all at once quite formal, "but I prefer that you do it."

He eyed her doubtfully for a moment and then with one eyebrow up and his voice commanding, he assented, "Very well, my girl, but be forewarned. I mean for you to drive my team into town tomorrow and learn how to handle them in traffic."

She put up her chin as she gave him the reins. "Oh, I know how to drive a team in traffic, make no mistake. I do not wish the responsibility of taking yours, that is all."

He said nothing to this, for Robby was bringing along the carriage he was driving, and grinning wildly. "Did you see there?"

"Where?" Bee looked around.

"There, by that green wagon," Robby announced in a high glee. "A performing bear! I saw it. I'm going there first."

Donna shook her head and looked heavenward. Fleetwood, who understood Robby's sentiments exactly, concurred, "It's a rare kick-up! Rare!"

Bee contemplated the two young men and laughed. "Frippery fellows. You be careful that bear doesn't see a good meal in you two."

"There's a rub." Connwood laughed and then, turning to look at Bee, said, "What do you wish to see first?"

"The fortune-teller," she answered promptly.

His lordship took the reins she held out to him

but pulled a face at her, clearly indicating that he thought she should have seen the job through and parked the phaeton. Fleetwood, still on his horse, led them toward the campsite, where, with much skill, Connwood situated his phaeton. Robby took a moment longer, for he found himself vying for position with an archaically styled coach. There was, in fact, every kind of vehicle present, from high-perched phaetons to weathered wagons. People meandered about the grounds, and the mood was festive.

Connwood found an urchin and cheerfully inquired whether the boy wanted to earn a coin watching his team. The youth quickly agreed to this, and his lordship dropped a coin into his dirty palm saying, "There will be another just like it when we return, so don't stray too far from their heads." He smiled at the lad and turned to help Bee down from the high perch. His hold on her trim waist lingered as she was set on ground, and his eyes twinkled at her as she blushed and lowered her gaze to her toes. Laughing out loud, he took her gloved hand and slipped it through his bent arm. "Come on, then, we have a carnival to attend."

She turned toward Fleetwood. "Yes, but George, Donna . . ." she objected as they moved away from their friends.

He didn't bother to look back, for he had already seen that Sir George was busy locating someone to take charge of his horse and that Robby and Donna had bumped into an old acquaintance.

"They'll all be along in a moment," he assured her happily. "Now, where would the fortune-teller be?"

A booth sporting dolls of various types caught Bee's attention, and she slipped out of his lordship's hold to move in its direction. He frowned at

61

this and followed her, smiling all at once when she held up a pretty china doll and exclaimed, much like a little girl, "Isn't she pretty?"

"Very, but not nearly—" he started.

She giggled. "Oh, don't say it." Shaking her head, she added, "It's much too pat."

"Monkey!" he chastized her and took up her hand. "Do you want it? Shall I purchase it for you?"

She was genuinely horrified. "Oh, no. Please, don't make me uncomfortable."

He was surprised. "Because I wish to give you some little gift? Don't be absurd, child."

She lowered her gaze again, and he shook his head and gave her a half smile. "Never mind. Come on, then."

She allowed him to hold her hand, although she was all too aware of his touch. What to do? Perhaps if she moved off and looked in at another booth, he would let her hand drop. Gently she moved to the right and with her free hand examined a small cameo on display.

"Do you want it?" His voice was soft and his eyes caressed.

She looked at him, and her fine brows drew together. This time she pulled her hand out of his and wagged a finger at him. "You must not. This is more unsuitable than the last. This is jewelry. Now stop, for I shan't be able to look at anything in your presence if you mean to try and buy everything I think is pretty."

"Yes, but if you like it . . . 'tis the veriest nothing—not really jewelry, I assure you. Bee, it's a trinket, and if you like it—"

She cut him off. "That doesn't mean I must have it, and if it was something I especially wanted, I am quite able to purchase it myself." She had partially turned her head, for the sound of music

62

caught her attention, and with an uplifted chin she said in some excitement, "Look, there is the fortune-teller!"

"And that, my girl, is something I mean to manage, and I want no arguments from you," he said very gravely.

She eyed him consideringly for a moment and then, biting her bottom lip, allowed, "Thank you, my lord."

Once again he took up her hand and they moved along. It was an incredible feeling, his hold on her small fingers, and she wondered if this was something he always did with women when escorting them. She looked up at his profile and asked, "Will you have your fortune read as well?"

He looked at her and said, "We'll see."

His lordship saw his charge comfortably situated and left her to her private reading. Standing just outside the Gypsy's wagon, he caught sight of Robby and waved.

"Come, John," Robby called. "Wait till you see this!"

Connwood looked back at the wagon's closed door and frowned, wondering if he had enough time, decided he wouldn't stay long with Robby, and moved through the busy throng of people to Robby's side.

Within the Gypsy's bright yellow painted wagon Lady Bee sat enthralled with the tarot cards being laid out before her. As the elderly woman spoke, Bee looked at her face and decided that the woman took her cards quite seriously and therefore put on a grave face and allowed the woman her moment.

"You are beloved," the woman said, and shook her head as she turned over yet another card, "but there will be hardships to face . . . soon." She sighed. "You plunge into danger . . ." She looked up and into Bee's eyes. "You are dedicated to your word, to your passion . . . and may suffer." Quickly the old woman turned over card after card and clucked. "Strife, everywhere you will find strife . . . Again here, you will find strife, danger, danger." She looked at Lady Bee and shrugged. "You are a young woman. Your gentleman perhaps wanted a light and happy reading for you. He will be angry."

"Nonsense. Life is full of ups and downs." Bee found herself attempting to assuage the woman's concerns.

"I can only tell you what the card says to me . . . that is all I can do." She shrugged her shoulders but looked intently at Bee. "You have a good heart. There are those that will hurt you."

Lady Bee had enough and got to her feet. "Thank you."

The Gypsy woman remained seated and inclined her head. "You are forewarned, if you believe."

Bee stepped into daylight and released the breath of air she had not even been aware she had been holding back. She looked around and did not see Robby and his lordship through the maze of passersby. She walked away from the crowded grassy aisle and moved toward a ring of horses, where she immediately pulled up short. That man! There was that dandy she had seen at the inn near Stonehenge.

Chapter Twelve

Mr. Holland prided himself on his wisdom. He was acutely aware and proud of a special sensitivity he believed he had. At the moment he fancied he felt someone staring at him and looked across to find Lady Bee doing just that. His brow went up, and as he immediately recognized her as the lovely young woman he had noticed at the Red Lion just yesterday, he inclined his head and touched the tip of his dark beaver top hat. A soft smile curved his thin lips, and he took a step in her direction.

Bee nearly panicked as she realized he was actually coming toward her. She turned and ran directly into Connwood's arms.

"Ho, my sweet." He laughed as he caught and held her. "Such frenzy? Did you miss me that much?"

"My lord, my lord," she breathed, "that man—" He had allowed her space enough to turn, though he held her still. She frowned, for the dandy was gone. "He was there . . . right there, I swear it."

"Who was, my love?" His lordship looked at her intently, for he could see she was disturbed.

She looked up at his face, released a long breath of air. "You must think me mad."

"I think you are adorable and upset about something. What is it?"

"It was just that I was so surprised when I saw him that I must have stared, and he caught me—staring, you see—and then he started toward me."

"Devil, you say!" His lordship's brow was up, and there was a touch of anger in his tone. "Who started for you?"

"That man. The one in the Red Lion yesterday. Do you remember?" She was frowning up at him again. "The dandy with the mustache."

He wanted to assuage her fears and found himself taking her chin. "Ah, the dandy."

She smiled sheepishly. "Yes, the dandy."

"No doubt when he caught sight of you again, my dear, he thought he might introduce himself. Then, when he saw you were escorted, he thought better of his designs."

"Yes, but—" She bit her lip, unable to go on.

"Yes, but what? Tell me, love," he urged and put her now into the crook of his arm.

"Nought. I am just being silly."

"You could never be silly. What is it?"

"Him . . . I suppose there is something about him that bothers me." She shrugged and released a short laugh. "Oh, I suppose it was just the fortune-teller. She may have rattled me. Spoke of my being in some sort of danger, you know."

"Did she, by God!" His lordship was clearly annoyed. "Well, perhaps I shall just go have a word with the woman."

She held his arm, "Oh, no, please do not. She meant no harm. Really, she was very nice to me."

"She frightened you." His lordship's lips were set in a hard, uncompromising line.

Lady Bee peeped up at him meekly. "If she did, 'twas my own fault for allowing myself to be so taken in. Please do not refine upon all this nonsense, for that is all it is. Come, let's go join Donna and the boys."

"Bound to be dull work tonight," Robby grumbled as he attempted to relax in his tight-fitting satin dress breeches.

"You look like you were poured into those." Fleetwood laughed. "You'd better talk to Byron and find out about that diet of his."

"Vinegar and potatoes," Donna said.

"Never say so!" Robby exclaimed in shocked accents. "Upon my soul." He shook his head. "Well, and I won't."

"Don't listen to Fleetie." Bee laughed. "You look fine. There isn't an ounce of fat on you. You look to me like you are all muscle."

"Well, my muscle will turn into fat, sitting around with a bunch of old biddies playing at whist." Robby pulled a grimace and turned to Donna. "I tell you what. Won't play whist."

"Whist?" Bee interjected. "I won't play whist, either." She turned to his lordship. "Is that what we were invited over to do? Play whist? I think I will develop a quinsy and go to my bed."

"Aye," Fleetwood agreed. "If it's whist your friends have in mind, think I'll stay home with Bee and Robby and play at ducks and drakes instead."

"Nonsensical children. Mary Russell said she was getting up a party for her houseguests and that there would be card tables set up for those who wished to play whist, but that she was also setting up the music room."

"Dancing, Bee," Fleetwood said, taking up her black velvet cloak and putting it around her shoulders. "Come on, then. We accept."

"Don't want to dance," Robby announced.

"Oh, Robby ..." Donna cajoled, stroking his white-gloved hand with exaggerated affection. "With me, Robby—don't you want to dance with me?"

He surveyed her face and relented, "Aye, with you but *not*," he added with emphasis, "with those old dowagers they are bound to throw at me."

Fleetwood turned and bent to pick up his own hat and cloak, and Bee found her eyes surveying John Connwood sadly. This time was nearly at an end. Soon her father would return to fetch her back to Saunders, and these days would only be memories. Look at him! So handsome with his ginger-gray silken waves framing his face and his eyes so rich with their bright blue color. His smile taunted her with his charm, and his charm mesmerized her heart. He was only passing time. He was only enjoying a mild flirtation. It meant nothing to him. Nothing at all.

"What are you doing, Bee? Daydreaming?" Fleetwood nudged her back to reality.

She saw her friend look between her and Connwood, who now had his back to them. Very little got by George Fleetwood, and she blushed. He lifted his brow and said quietly, "Just so. Quite out of your range, my dear."

"Yes, I know," she answered in a voice that was scarcely audible.

Mary Russell's soiree was already festively in progress when Lord Connwood and his party arrived on the scene. Robby grumbled beneath his breath until his Donna popped a substantial tidbit from a passing tray into his mouth. He announced this to be unquestionably delicious and went in search of more. Fleetwood discovered two of his hunting cronies and fell into lively banter with them. Champagne flowed, and Mary Russell's guests all seemed disposed to a genial evening.

Lady Bee was introduced to one of the gray-haired dowagers, a sweet-tempered older woman who related an anecdote involving Bee's father. It was some moments later, and just as Bee was hoping she could rejoin her friends, that the dowager clucked and offered, "Oh, now listen to me. There I go on and on, when your pretty little feet must be itching to be on the dance floor. Go on. No doubt Connwood"—she indicated with her uplifted brow and the cock of her head—"over there is anxiously awaiting your return."

Bee rose, thanked her, told her she would be sure to carry her regards to her father, and started toward his lordship, who was indeed looking her way.

"Finally," said a male's casual voice at her back.

Lady Bee turned in puzzlement and instinctively took a step backward, for here was the dandy. Mr. Holland repeated, this time more softly, "Finally we meet, and what pleasant circumstances." He held himself up. "Ah, perhaps I should observe the proprieties and fetch my cousin, Mary, to introduce us."

"Mary Russell? Mrs. Russell is your cousin?" Bee was surprised into asking.

"Indeed, Lady Barbara, our mothers were sisters, you see." He spoke to her as though she were a child. He inclined his head slightly. "And I am Felix Holland."

She couldn't help but be astonished. "How did you know my name?"

"I made it my business to find out who you were as soon as I saw you walk into the ballroom. I also know that you and your father, the Earl of Saunders, are guests in Lord Connwood's home."

"No doubt you think you are being very suave and clever, but I find you impertinent."

Mr. Holland was not used to such treatment. His eyes narrowed, and he decided the chit wanted discipline. Such retaliation was, however, forestalled as Connwood appeared suddenly. His lordship nodded politely toward Holland, but there was no mistaking the dismissal in his eyes as he then turned to take up Lady Bee's bare elbow and lead her off,

"I have asked for a waltz to be struck up," he whispered softly as he bent to her ear.

"Oh, my lord," Bee almost wailed, "I don't know if I can waltz with you."

"Why ever not?" His blue eyes opened wide.

"Well, I have never waltzed with anyone other than my father and Fleetie, and then I don't think I was terribly graceful."

He laughed. "Just let yourself go ... feel the pressure of my hands."

Oh, how she felt the pressure on her waist, on her gloved hand—how wonderful, how protected she felt. She couldn't meet his gaze. She heard him chuckle, and her eyes flashed as they discovered the twinkle in his.

"Don't laugh at me, my lord; I am minding my steps."

"I am not laughing *at* you, my sweet thing. I find you adorable, and as to minding your steps, you are doing very well." He nodded to another couple. "I think we are doing rather better than Donna and Robby."

She glanced in their direction and giggled. "Hmm. But they are so cute." She sighed and then frowned as her glance happened to find Mr. Holland standing on the sidelines looking her way.

"He frightens me."

"Who, Holland?" Connwood was serious now, and his eyes scanned her face.

"Yes. How do you know his name?" Bee's eyes were opened wide.

"I saw him approach you and inquired," his lordship answered her simply.

"Oh." Bee sighed, pleased enough with his answer. "Well, he introduced himself. He said he knew who I was. He said he knew my father and I were your guests at Searington." She bit her lip. "He—oh, I don't know—but he makes me feel uncomfortable. There is something about the way he looks at me."

Connwood held her tighter. "My love, you are a beautiful little thing. Men are going to look at you. It is something you will have to get used to and eventually enjoy, not too much, I hope." He was smiling down at her with some affection.

She peeped at him in a style all her own. "Oh, my lord, I am not so green as that. You look at me. Fleetie sometimes looks at me, but not quite the way Holland looks at me." She shook her head. "There is something sinister about him."

Connwood laughed. "No, my love. His name is an old one, and to the best of my knowledge, Felix Holland has never stirred up more than the usual scandals."

"Usual? What is usual?"

"Oh, gambling away what little inheritance he had . . . drinking more than he should on auspicious occasions," Connwood answered flippantly, for he thought little of such absurdities.

"What auspicious occasions?" Bee inquired with genuine curiosity.

"What difference does it make?" He looked at her reprovingly.

"It might. What auspicious occasions? Some major event, for comments to be made, evidently."

"Aye, I suppose. He thought he was going to come into his uncle's inheritance about a year or so ago. Instead, his uncle willed the bulk of his estate to Felix's young cousin, can't think of the boy's name. Felix displayed himself to disadvantage, the rumour has it. However, seems to have made up with the family, taken the boy—orphaned I think—under his wing. I only know the story from Mary. This is the first I have encountered Holland." He looked at Bee. "There, now do you feel better?"

She smiled at him. "I suppose . . ."

He held her tighter. "Mind your steps, my lady."

Chapter Thirteen

The Earl of Saunders arrived while Connwood was merrily entertaining his guests over the breakfast table. He was announced and strode into the room, putting out his arms for his daughter, who had jumped to her feet and skipped the short distance between them.

"Papa!" Bee threw her arms round his neck. "I am so happy you are here. I have missed you."

"Have you, brat? I hear quite different from Sir George. I met him down the drive. He tells me you have been having a busy time of it."

She giggled. "I wish Fleetie didn't have to leave already, but I did miss you."

"I don't think you even knew I was gone." He embraced her warmly once more and smiled at the assembled company, all waving from the table, Robby with buttered toast in hand.

Bee slapped playfully at his upper arm as she stood away from him. "Fie, Papa, how can you say such a thing?"

"Because you looked content enough." He laughed at her.

"And so I was. You know I always make the best of whatever fate deals me." She giggled deliciously.

"Ho! I agree with your father. You are a brat. Making the best of it, are you? And here I thought you were enjoying my hospitality." Connwood shook his head sadly.

She threw a shoulder and a coy look at him. "And so I have enjoyed your, er, hospitality, my dear lord."

"Minx," his lordship answered softly now and touched her pert nose. He turned to the earl. "Come, sir, join us for breakfast, for we have only just started, and you must be hungry after your ride."

"Yes, I shall, and perhaps we may between us decide what *fate* my girl shall next have to manage."

"Oh, Papa, that is really too bad of you," his daughter bantered in return and saw him comfortably seated beside her at the table.

"Is it, and so you shall say when I tell you that I mean to take you directly home right after we have breakfasted."

Her smile vanished, and she couldn't stop the sound as it came to her lips, "No, oh, no," and then with a blush she added, "So soon?"

"I think we should before we have outlived our welcome here. I am certain his lordship has better things to do than wait on us at Searington," her father reproved gently.

"We, too," Donna said. "If you leave, then so shall we."

"What is this?" his lordship put in immediately. "Everyone leaving the ship? I rather thought my guests were well pleased with my attentions."

"More than pleased," the earl responded at once, "but I can't call on your kindness any longer."

"It is *your* kindness, my lord, for allowing me to

host you at Searington," Connwood returned immediately and at his most charming.

The earl laughed heartily all at once. "I can see that I am well met, but the truth is, I am off to London. You know I plan to give Bee a season and must see to the opening of our town house."

"Yes, but Missy—" Bee started.

"Is sound enough to make a slow journey home, puss, and well you know. I have it from the stables that you were on her back late yesterday afternoon and that she was quite a handful."

"Yes, Papa," Bee said sadly, looking at the toes of her yellow silk slippers. She knew from his tone that he would not brook any further argument from her now.

"Well, this is exciting. I didn't know that you were planning a London season for Bee," Connwood said at this juncture, his charm still in his smile. "But what of that mare of yours? She should be left here at Searington until she comes into heat."

"Yes, I mean to send her over with my man. Looks as though she is very nearly ready."

"Good, good, but then . . . why not leave Bee here? After all, Donna and Robby are staying on with me another few days, and Bee would enjoy it. She'll do better here chaperoned by Donna than alone at home while you are in London." Connwood spoke softly, but he could see the earl was not quite satisfied with this suggestion. He added, "But of course you must do what you feel is best."

Here was the rub. Donna and Robby Huxley were a respectable couple, and Donna's position as a married lady offered a chaperon for Bee. However, Donna was not only Bee's friend, she was younger than Bee. Therefore, how could Donna count as a chaperon for Bee for more than a few days? He looked at his daughter. She was looking radiant in her yellow muslin morning gown, with her tawny curls in wild profusion around her piquant face. She looked happy. He adored her, and she deserved to be happy. If he took her home, she would do well enough, but Connwood was right; she would be left to her own devices. Such had been the case since her dear mother's death so many years ago. Right, then, he would cut his London trip down to the bone.

He turned to Donna. "I can't believe I am saying this to you, for your scrapes have often numbered in one week slightly more than Bee's; however, I shall leave you to oversee my daughter." He turned to Robby. "And I hold you responsible for both these chits, and make no mistake, it is a terrifying occupation. I pity you, my boy."

Robby looked quite horrified but squared his shoulders. "Don't worry about it, my lord. I'll make sure they don't kick up a dust while you're gone."

The earl glanced his way ruefully and said on a dry note, "Well, if you manage that, it will be more than I was able to do over the last nineteen years."

Nineteen. The word stuck in Connwood's mind for a moment as he looked at Bee. She was only nineteen. He was a good ten years older than she. So pretty standing there, with her gray eyes twinkling. She would have her London season, meet some eligible bachelor, and off she would go. He would, during the course of the London season, formally propose to Lady Sarah. Egad! Lady Sarah! This was the first time in days that her name had come to mind. He frowned.

"Well, look at you," Bee giggled at Connwood. "Now that it is all settled, you are looking glum."

He gave her a half smile. "Aye, thought your papa would hold out and save me, but alas . . ."

"Wretch." She pulled at the silky hair at the nape of his neck before seating herself at the table. "Hmm. Donna, would you pass me the marmalade? I am suddenly ravenous."

Connwood sipped his coffee but pushed his food about on his plate, having momentarily lost his appetite. Marriage? It was something he had promised his family he would take on so that a suitable heir would be produced to carry on the name, the tradition. The Lady Sarah had been chosen for him, and he had been satisfied enough with the choice . . . so what, then, was the rub?

"When do you think they will return?" Bee asked Donna as they trotted their horses across the open field.

"Oh, I don't know. Robby said they would probably go to a local tavern after the cock fight." She pulled a face and hunched her shoulders as she cringed at the thought of cock fighting. "Ugh, Bee, it is the most horrible thing. How can they? I mean, how can they watch those poor creatures pluck themselves to death?"

"Not themselves, Donna, each other, and there is no sense asking a question like that, for we could never really understand the answer. I mean, men do watch and wager on the outcome of a man beating another man senseless, you know. Sport, my dear. There is no sense in it, but there it is, sport." Bee grimaced and then groaned, "Oh, no."

"Oh, no, what?" Donna looked in the direction of Bee's glance to see a man riding toward them dressed in some elegant finery quite overdone for the hour and the country. Beside him was a female

77

rider, Mary Russell. " 'Tis your beau." Donna giggled suddenly.

"Wretch, how can you tease me about such a thing when you know he positively frightens me?" Bee returned sharply.

"Well, as to that, you are being absurd," Donna said reasonably. "Why should he frighten you? Besides, Mary Russell is with him and I am with you, so consider yourself well protected." Donna was teasing, but all Bee could do was give her a half smile.

They pulled up their horses and awaited the arrival of the two riders. Mary Russell waved her crop at them, and Bee could see already that something was wrong by the set of her full mouth. "Oh, my dears, we were just on our way to see you at Searington."

"Good morning, ladies." Mr. Holland nodded his well-shaped head, and Donna thought fleetingly that he was rather good-looking in a florid manner.

"Well, then I am glad we have not missed you. Shall we ride back to Searington together?" Bee offered, dearly hoping Mrs. Russell would decline.

"Is Lord Connwood there, then?" Mary Russell's fine brows were drawn together still.

"No, he is out for the day." Bee looked at her a moment before gently inquiring, "Is . . . is there something we could do? Is something wrong?"

"Oh, I don't know if there is anything you can do, though you can relay a message to him." She turned to Holland. "Isn't that right, Felix? I might as well tell the girls—the more people that know, the more help it might be in the end. One never knows who has seen what."

"Mrs. Russell, I don't understand. What has occurred to overset you like this?" Bee pursued.

"Indeed, Mary, you might as well tell the girls, though I don't know what more than gossip will be accomplished," Holland said, obviously irritated.

"These girls will not gossip, and as I said, perhaps in the end it will be a help." She turned to them, "My little cousin has disappeared."

Chapter Fourteen

"Your little cousin?" Bee asked, puzzled. "I don't think I understand."

"No, of course not," Felix Holland answered, playing with his cravat. "How could you?" He turned impatiently to Mary Russell. "Really, Mary . . ."

She ignored him and went on to explain, "My young cousin, Thomas Holland . . . he is only ten, and he inherited his father's estates, fortune, and title." She shook her head. "Little Sir Thomas, poor boy—he is orphaned, and his father's will only provided for him financially, you see. No guardian was named . . . well, one had been when the will was originally written, but that gentleman has died since that time."

"Mary, they don't need to be burdened with all this," Felix interjected impatiently. "They were out for a lovely morning ride, and here we are absolutely distressing them."

"No, please, do go on," Bee urged, moving her horse closer to Mary.

"Yes, I just wanted you to understand," Mary apologized with a half smile directed at the girls, "how the family decided to leave him with Augusta Penistone. You see, she was his aunt and godmother and had always been with him . . . well, at least for the last five years, since his mother's death . . . and he adored her. She is getting on in years, as Felix had pointed out to us so often, but she seemed the best candidate for the job. She is his aunt, after all, and childless. Well, we thought—"

"And were damned wrong." Felix interrupted again. "Oh, do please excuse my rudeness, but I felt strongly at the time, and look what has come of it."

"Yes, well . . . Augusta lives near young Sir Thomas's estate and rather than move in with him, she took him to her home, which is only two miles from Holland House. The boy was happy there; really, he had no wish to run off. I know, for I visited him often, and he was happy—"

"Yet he has run off," Felix cut her off.

"No, no, I refuse to believe that." She frowned at Felix. "He is an active little fellow, forever escaping from his tutor if he can, but why would he run away from home? I fear that someone has abducted him for ransom." She ended on a breathless note.

"Has a request for ransom been delivered to Lady Penistone or to the family?" Donna inquired quietly.

"No." Mary Russell was frowning. "That is what puzzles us so. But we only just discovered he was missing. Perhaps a note for ransom is still forthcoming."

"I don't understand. You only just discovered he is missing? Please explain."

"Lady Penistone had written that he wanted to visit with Mr. Russell and me. We have always adored Thomas, and he so enjoys our son, John, who is only a year younger than . . . but let me not digress. It was decided that we would allow him to travel to us with a friend of Lady Penistone's who was traveling through the vicinity. We expected her to arrive with Thomas yesterday afternoon. When we didn't hear from them, we just thought they were delayed. 'Tis no more than a half day's journey, though, and I was rather upset, but Mr. Russell said I was being nonsensical."

She shook her head over it. "I wasn't being nonsensical, though. I knew it, felt it. Deep inside I knew something was not right. Then she arrived today, the awful creature, and she did not have Thomas with her."

"Faith." Bee breathed, touched with an impatience to get to the meat of the story. "What do you mean? She didn't bring your young cousin?"

"No, she lost him." Again she shook her head. "They stopped for refreshments two hours after they had left Penistone, and Thomas went into the courtyard to have a go with some animal or other, and he vanished. Mrs. Woxly—the woman he was traveling with—nearly suffered a stroke when it dawned on her that he was nowhere in the inn. She sent for the local magistrate, who instituted an immediate search of the area, but no one had even seen any boy fitting Thomas's description. Mrs. Woxly came to us this morning in an absolute state of hysteria."

Donna and Bee exchanged glances, and cautiously Bee inquired, "Mrs. Russell, who besides your husband, yourself, and Lady Penistone, knew that your cousin was traveling with this woman to your home?"

"Well, I don't know . . . no one of any import. It was such a last-minute plan." She shook her head. "Do you suspect foul play?"

"Don't be so melodramatic." Felix was again impatient.

"I don't know. Who stood to inherit if anything happened to your cousin?" Bee asked.

"You are direct," Felix said in a suddenly low, strange voice.

"A besetting sin," Bee answered, meeting his gaze with her cool gray eyes.

"I am not sure. No one really knows," Mary Russell answered.

"Explain," Bee returned, "if you don't mind, for I think it might mean something."

"Sir Thomas was an only child, and of course had no heirs. Unless his father stipulated a specific survivor in his son's stead, well—" she looked at Holland—"I suppose it would be Augusta Penistone. She is, after all, Thomas's aunt, Holland's sister."

Mrs. Russell dug into the small leather saddle bag and pulled out a miniature, handing it to Lady Bee. "This is a good likeness of Thomas. I had it done of the boys when Thomas was with us three months ago. The taller, fair-haired boy is Thomas."

Bee looked at the face of Thomas Holland and nearly choked. She controlled herself and managed to swallow the exclamation that sprang to her lips. When she looked up, it was to find Felix's hazel eyes narrowing as he surveyed her face.

"Thank you. I will certainly keep my ears open and help in anyway I can." She turned and handed the miniature to Donna, who looked it over, repeated much the same, and returned it to Mrs. Russell.

Bee and Donna took their leave, and it was with some excitement that Donna demanded as soon as they were out of earshot, "What?"

83

Bee looked at her, "What do you mean, what?"

"I saw your face, Bee. You recognized that boy. Now tell me what is going on." Donna was nearly shrieking.

"Donna, that was the face of the little boy in that Gypsy wagon I saw—I swear, 'tis the same face!"

Chapter Fifteen

"Oh, my faith!" Donna's voice was certainly high-pitched. "What are we going to do?"

Bee was biting her lip in a way peculiar to herself, for her thoughts were racing and tumbling into one another. She looked at her friend and said thoughtfully, "I am surprised that it is Lady Penistone who inherits. I would have put this at Felix Holland's door."

"Hmm. Yes, but—"

"And he was at that inn where I saw the Gypsy wagon and that boy. There is more to this, and I tell you, Donna, Felix is behind it, I'm sure."

"Yes, but—"

"You know what we have to do?" It was not really meant as a question.

"Yes, but, Bee—"

"But, Bee? But, Bee, what?"

"We should wait for Robby at least." Donna knew what Bee had in her head. They had been friends a long time.

"Wish we could, but who knows when they will return, and then they won't believe our woman's intuition, and besides, we will only go discover if we are right. Then we can send them in if we are."

Donna frowned and made one more attempt to

curb her friend. "Bee, think . . . we might be running off on a wild-goose chase, and no one even knows where we are off to. Shouldn't we ride back to Searington first?"

"Donna, since when are you so fainthearted? There isn't time. Right now, that caravan might be packing up and going off. We have to ride, and fast, now, while our horses are fresh."

"Yes, but what if they have left already?" Donna was quickly losing reasonable objections and knew that, in truth, she wanted to rush off with Bee in this heady fashion.

"Then we'll find out in which direction they went. That shouldn't be too hard." Bee looked at her for a long moment. "You could ride back to Searington and wait for Robby."

Donna put a hand on her hip. "Get going, girl!"

Bee smiled. "Right." She giggled and spurred her horse into an instant canter.

"Mad, you are absolutely mad." Donna laughed, riding with her.

The Gypsies had packed their tents and looked as though they would soon be hitching up their horses to their wagons and leaving. Bee was biting her bottom lip and thinking as she sat her horse and watched from the vantage point they had chosen in the woods adjacent to the camp.

"Donna . . . there, see that green-and-yellow wagon just outside the circle of wagons?"

"Yes, is that it?" Donna was excited and the tremor in her whisper displayed this.

"Yes, I think so."

"Well, what are we going to do?" Donna inquired on a low note.

"I think we will ride right up to the caravan, close to the green wagon, and dismount."

"What? Why?" Donna was shrieking.

"Well, for goodness' sake, it is broad daylight. We can't just sneak up on the wagon in broad daylight, so we'll have to do as much as we can in the open, distract them—I don't know, we'll play it by ear."

"Oh, mercy," Donna wailed.

"Hmm. Come, we'll keep our horses as close as we can after we dismount, just in case."

"Just in case? Just in case, what?"

"I don't know. Just in case," Bee answered impatiently and started out of the woods.

"Oh, God," Donna wailed, and followed her.

No one seemed to pay too much attention to them as they arrived at the circle of wagons and dismounted their horses. Bee spoke idly to a Gypsy woman packing her trinkets and, in fact, made her grin happily as she purchased a piece. She then turned to Donna and whispered, "Take my reins."

"What? What are you doing?" Donna demanded as she took Missy's reins and held both horses at her back.

"Sh." Bee had put a finger to her lips and vanished behind a wagon, leaving Donna with the horses.

Quickly and without being noticed, she managed the short distance to the bright green wagon. There was no one about, and without hesitation she climbed the one rear step and tried the door. Her brows went up as the door swung open, for she had not expected it to be so easy. She nearly jumped inside and closed the door at her back.

Hunched in a corner of the cluttered wagon, his hands bound behind his back and his feet bound at the ankles before him, was a young boy. His blue eyes opened wide when he saw Bee, but he couldn't speak, as a cloth had been stuffed into his mouth.

Bee went directly to him and got to her knees as she gently pulled the cloth from his sore little mouth.

"There, you poor young thing . . . sh, don't speak. Sir Thomas, we must get you out of here."

"He—he will be back," the boy said hoarsely.

Bee worked the knots at his feet and attempted to assuage the boy's fears. "Yes, I am sure he—whoever he is—will be back, and when he does come back, he will have quite a bit to answer for."

"No, no, he is horrible. He will kill us, means to kill me, I know," the child said, his eyes wild with fright.

"Sh, love. If he meant to kill you, he would have done so. You see, we needn't worry." Bee tugged at the stubborn knot, wishing it would come undone. It stayed firm, and she broke two of her nails. "Drat!"

"Can't kill me till we're out of the county. Heard him tell someone that he wants to wait, but he will if he has to, I can tell," Sir Thomas said. "I'm so tired, miss."

"Of course you are. There!" Bee could have shouted with glee as she got the knot binding around his ankles undone and pulled him forcefully to his feet. "Stand, Sir Thomas. You can do it. Please stand."

He pulled himself up bravely, though his knees were stiff and nearly bent beneath his light weight. "I am sorry, miss. You must think me—"

"An amazingly strong young man . . . beyond your years. I would be proud if you were my brother. Come, we'll do your wrists when we are away from this wagon." She put her arm round his small waist and helped him to the door. Donna, Donna, she thought to herself, be near—please be near and ready.

As though Donna had read her mind, anticipated her needs, she was scarcely twenty feet away looking as though she were merely grazing the horses. She saw Bee with the boy almost at once and breathed out loud, "Faith, he really was there. Faith—oh, my goodness." She jogged the horses toward Bee.

"Hold there!" screamed a man's voice at Bee's back. She turned and saw a round, large dark man in brightly colored clothes hobbling toward them.

Without a word between them, they worked like a team. Donna held Missy still while Bee hoisted the boy on the count of three into the saddle. She then pulled herself onto her horse's back, sitting on her poor mare's kidneys. It was a tight fit with the boy in the saddle before her, but she managed to click the mare off as Donna mounted her already moving gelding. They were off in a flash and rushing the woods without looking back. Bee held the boy around his waist, as his hands were still tied at his back, and she managed her horse with her free hand until they arrived at the open post road and slowed to a trot.

"Did he follow us, do you think?" Donna asked breathlessly.

"I very much doubt it," Bee said, pulling a face. "What could he do, claim we have stolen his property? His son? What?"

"Yes, but he thinks we are unattended. He might—"

"By now he is taking his wagon, leaving his caravan, and making his escape. Donna, he has no doubt already been paid and has no reason to risk his neck. Why would he pursue us to the open road?" She touched Thomas's hair and asked gently, "Sir Thomas, do you know who gave you over to the Gypsy?"

"No, I only know that the Gypsy grabbed me and threw me into his wagon. He tied me up, and when I made a fuss, he stuffed my mouth with that dirty rag. I—why would he do such a thing?"

"Never mind. Don't you think about it. We'll have you returned to your family in no time."

"Was it my Aunt Gussie?" Sir Thomas felt a tear well up and spill over. "Doesn't my Aunt Gussie want me anymore?"

"Your Aunt Gussie loves you. Why would you think such a thing?"

"She wanted me to go to my cousin Mary because she wanted me out of the way while she got married again, that's why," he said on a sad note.

Donna and Bee exchanged glances, and Bee said softly, "Wanting a little private time to be with a new husband does not mean your aunt does not love you. Adults are like that when they want to be romantic and mushy, you know." She smiled at him, tilting his face to look at her as she did so, for she had pulled Missy to a stop. "Understand?"

He grinned suddenly, for this made sense to him and he wanted to believe his Aunt Augusta loved him still. "Yes, I suppose so."

"Good. Now, I think we'll take you to Searington and get you washed and fed before we send for your cousin Mary. How is that?"

"Yes, please, but could I be fed and then washed?"

Donna and Bee laughed out loud, pleased to see his spirit still in place. "Yes, you may be fed and then washed. Lord, definitely washed," Bee answered, ruffling his hair once more.

Chapter Sixteen

Young Sir Thomas was abovestairs enjoying his bath. The girls had been satisfied as they watched him devour a considerable quantity of food before they gave him over to Connwood's startled valet.

Bee put down her half-finished cup of tea and sighed, for there was a problem presenting itself to her. "Donna, what are we going to do?"

Donna started to worry. "What do you mean? What have you got groping around in that brain of yours?"

"How can you be so dense?" Bee returned impatiently. "We can't just send him back to Mary Russell."

"She didn't send him to the Gypsies." Donna stopped as dawning lit her face with horror. "Bee, what are we going to do?"

"Exactly," Bee answered, pleased to have her friend recognize the problem.

"Devil a bit!" exclaimed Robby as he strode into the dining room and moved to put an arm around his wife. "Heard you two have been running amok. What's toward?"

"What have you been told?" Bee asked, her eyes flying to Connwood's countenance as he followed

Robby into the room and came toward her, his glance taking in her disheveled appearance.

"We were told at the stables that you came in riding double with a young boy and that your horses had been ridden hard," Connwood answered. "From your riding habits, I fear you were doing more than riding at a heady pace," Connwood said quietly. "Indulge me and start at the beginning."

"It's complicated," Donna answered, attempting to gather her thoughts.

"Sir Thomas was the boy I saw the other day in that Gypsy wagon, and Felix Holland is the one who arranged it. We saved Sir Thomas, and he is upstairs with your valet in the bath." Bee saw that both men were looking bewildered, so she favored them with a further explanation. "Well, Sir Thomas is in the bath, and your valet is seeing to him."

Connwood and Robby exchanged glances, and Connwood prompted patiently, "Sir Thomas, I take it, is the young man you rode double with on your poor Missy." There was the reprove in his tone.

"Yes, we rode double, but we had no choice, now, did we? And besides, Missy held up perfectly, and we slowed to a walk as soon as we knew we weren't followed."

"Followed by whom?" Connwood asked in some surprise.

"By the Gypsies. Don't you understand? No, of course not. You weren't there this morning when Mary Russell and Felix Holland met us in the upper field and Mrs. Russell told us that Sir Thomas had been abducted. Well, at least we didn't know he was abducted, for there wasn't a ransom note, but he had disappeared while he was on his way to stay with her while his aunt got used to her new husband. Well, we decided that it was Felix Holland who abducted him. We don't know why yet, though we have our suspicions, and we decided that he was in the green Gypsy wagon, so we went to the caravan. . . ." She paused for breath.

"You went by yourselves to the Gypsy caravan?" Robby nearly screeched, so high-pitched was his voice.

"Had to," Bee answered softly. "There was no telling when they would pack up their supplies and leave, and they were, in fact, taking down their tents when we rode up. Well, never mind. We had no choice, and Donna held the horses while I managed to sneak into the wagon—"

"You went into the wagon?" Connwood asked on a grave note, his eyes scanning her face with something of wonder.

"Well, what else could I do? Poor little thing was there, stuffed into a corner with a rag in his mouth, his ankles and wrists bound, thinking all manner of things."

"Yes, but, Bee, why didn't you wait for us?" Connwood demanded quietly.

"There wasn't time. As it was, I just managed to get his ties undone round his ankles and off we had to run, with this dreadful man at our heels."

"Man? A man chased you?" Robby swung round on this, and it was obvious he was most distressed. He looked at his lordship. "Someone needs blood-letting—*now*!"

"Yes, Robby, and we will have his blood, perhaps all of it before we are done, but first we need some facts," Connwood answered, his blue eyes hard, his voice low and dangerous. "Go on, my little one. What, then, did you do?"

Bee watched Donna rub her cheek against Robby's arm and had a moment's urge to feel Connwood's arm go round her. She controlled the momentary lapse and proceeded. "What could we

93

do? We ran. Donna was right there with the horses, for she knew just what to do, and we threw poor Thomas up, mounted, and bolted out of there."

Connwood moved to her and bent to his knee, taking her hands from her lap and holding them both to his lips. "Unhurt? Are you unhurt?"

"Of course." She smiled at him. "Afraid of my father's wrath?"

He shook his head. "Not your father's, my girl, my own. There is none like to my own."

She frowned over this, unsure as to his meaning, and urged him to get back to his feet. "Please, my lord . . ."

He did, and took a turn about the room. Robby was petting his wife and announced suddenly, "Famous! Up to every rig, our girls! These two are complete hands!" It was obvious that he was quite proud.

"Yes, and now what is to be done?" Connwood was playing with his bottom lip.

"What do you mean, what should be done?" Robby was frowning. "The girls must have sent word to the boy's guardian?" He looked at Donna, who shook her head. "No? You haven't? But why on earth not?"

"They were quite right not to," Connwood said quietly. He paced a moment and then looked at Bee. "We will have to handle this delicately."

"Hmm, but on further reflection, I rather think that Holland would not dare play his game while the boy is within easy access. He wouldn't want suspicion cast his way."

"Perhaps, but I think we might take it one step further," Connwood said. "Send your note, Bee— Mary Russell shouldn't be kept from the news another minute longer."

"Yes, but what are you going to do? What step further?" Bee demanded curiously.

"Ah, some things are better left unspoken," he answered glibly and moved to pull the bell rope.

"Ha!" Bee exclaimed, outraged. "This was our adventure, and we have a right to know."

"Debatable. What you have a right to is a severe lecture from your papa when he returns and finds that you have forced poor Donna to be a part of your wild doings," his lordship returned easily.

Bee jumped to her feet, hands on hips, and objected with some heat, "I am going to my room!"

"I think not, brat," his lordship said, his eyes twinkling. "You have a note to write, I believe." He turned then to the butler, who had arrived in answer to his call on the rope a moment earlier and requested writing material be brought to the dining room.

"I can write it from my room," Bee declared pugnaciously.

"I am sure you can, but you will not do so." Connwood's eyes were steely as he gave her look for look.

Lady Bee pounced back into her chair. Donna looked from his lordship to her friend, burst out laughing, and took a slice of apple from her plate and popped it into her husband's open mouth.

Chapter Seventeen

The letter to Mary Russell had been drawn in Bee's hand, but it was his lordship who did the composing. Carefully, slowly, he had dictated to Lady Bee, and so pleased was she with the results that she nearly forgot to be put out with him. The men retired to the study, and the girls rushed upstairs to bathe and change before Mary Russell and Felix Holland's arrival.

Some sixty minutes later both girls were looking their best and fidgeting about the study as Robby and his lordship quietly discussed the latest piece of farm machinery. Lady Bee nearly stomped her foot when she addressed a question to his lordship and he merely responded that she was being missish.

"Missish?" Clearly Lady Bee was outraged. "How can you say so?"

He looked at her. She was a darling, in her white muslin with the red velvet flecks throughout and the red bow in her tawny locks. Her eyes were clear and sparkling, and he found her beautiful. He relented and said, "Missish? Did I say such a thing? How stupid I am sometimes."

She raised a brow and unconsciously moved toward him, "You are never stupid, and I am *not* missish."

He laughed out loud and acceded the point. "But, my dear, you *are* quite, quite lovely."

She managed a smile before her attention was taken by a small knock at the open door. There stood young Sir Thomas, clean and fed but still looking the worse for wear, since, having no other clothes, he had been forced to redon his soiled garments,

"Hallo," he said from the doorway.

"Thomas," Bee called, "come in here and meet Mr. Huxley and Lord Connwood." She got up and went up to him, her hand outstretched.

He gave her his hand and looked up at her adoringly as he moved into the room. Bee ruffled his hair and said that he looked fine. He wrinkled his nose and said, "Aw, no Lady Bee, my clothes smell as though I was rolling in—"

"You'll do." Bee laughed, cutting him off and then introducing him to the two men.

They had scarcely enjoyed a moment's conversation with the lad when the Searlington butler announced Mrs. Russell. She nearly ran into the room when she spied Sir Thomas and scooped him up thankfully into her arms. Bee watched her for a moment and sighed happily to see that the woman was sincerely attached to the boy before she realized that Holland was not present. This dawned on her, and she turned to meet Connwood's eyes. He was looking thoughtful.

Bee moved closer to him and cautiously, confidingly, leaned into his shoulder. "My lord, my lord—"

He answered her on a hushed note, "Yes, love, I know," and then turned to Mrs. Russell,

"Seems to be a plucky lad, been through an ordeal but doesn't seem any the worse for wear."

"Yes, yes," Mary Russell thankfully breathed, "but tell me, how, where . . ." She was teary-eyed as she held Thomas tightly and attempted to compose herself.

"It was Bee," Donna answered. "She remembered seeing him the other day in a Gypsy wagon." Donna's last words were touched with doubt as she caught Bee's warning glare.

Unobtrusively Connwood took hold. Felix Holland was not present, but it wouldn't do for him to hear this and later realize that Bee had seen Sir Thomas at the same inn where she had seen him. Dangerous.

"As it happens, we were at the carnival, and Bee did see his face at the window, but only for a moment. It struck Bee as odd, for he didn't have a Gypsy-like appearance. He was fair, blue-eyed. Then you came upon the girls this morning, and when you told them of your young cousin's disappearance, they impulsively played a hunch and returned to the Gypsy caravan where they did indeed find young Thomas."

"Mary . . . they were wonderful," Thomas said, staring from Bee to Donna worshipfully. "Lady Bee got me loose, and Mrs. Huxley had horses waiting just outside, just like any of the best stories I have ever read."

Mary Russell put a hand to her forehead. "I am so thankful to you—to all of you—but I am at a loss to understand. Mr. Russell will return this evening, and I am sure he will instigate proceedings against these Gypsies and perhaps get to the bottom of this."

"Exactly so," his lordship approved. "In the meantime, why don't you sit and take some tea with us?" Already his lordship's man was setting out a tray.

"No, no, I thought I would take Thomas home straightaway. Mr. Russell will be home soon, and I thought it would be best if I were there to give him the news. My son is anxiously awaiting Thomas's arrival as well, and I think it will be good for Thomas to see him."

"Oh, yes, please," Thomas agreed at once.

"Of course," his lordship answered, and moved to give her escort. "No doubt Felix will be at Russell Place awaiting your return?"

"No, dear Felix said he would ride to Augusta at once and relieve her mind. I think from there he travels back to London."

"How kind of Mr. Holland," put in Lady Bee, who had walked with Mrs. Russell toward the door. She touched Sir Thomas's head fondly and said, "It only surprises me that he did not wait long enough to see his young cousin for himself."

"Don't like Felix," Sir Thomas said pugnaciously. "Glad he isn't here."

"Thomas!" Mrs. Russell objected.

"Oh, never mind. We can't like everyone, now, can we?" Bee returned, making light of the subject. She bent and dropped a kiss on young Tom's nose. "I shall see you soon."

He threw his arms round her at once. "Yes, please."

Donna went to him at this point. "I don't mean to let you leave without giving me one of those nice hugs of yours."

He eyed the ground a moment and then his face lit with a smile. "Aw . . ." So declaring himself, he relented and gave Donna a bear hug as well before turning and slipping his hand into Mary Russell's open palm.

The assembled company waited only a moment after their departure before turning once more to one another. Questions flew from all, and they were directed toward his lordship.

"Why didn't Felix come with Mrs. Russell?" Donna asked.

"Why did you let that little chap go off with her, with that Felix fellow lurking about?" Robby wanted to know.

"Why didn't you want me to tell about being there that day with Felix Holland and the Gypsy wagon? Bee saw Holland, and she saw Sir Thomas in the Gypsy wagon. Doesn't that mean something? Shouldn't we have warned Mrs. Russell?" Donna asked.

"My lord"—Bee said his name softly before he had a chance to answer the barrage of questions—"what shall we do to protect Thomas from Holland?"

He touched her cheek. "I mean to meet with Mr. Russell tonight, after he has had a chance to see his wife. We can't very well throw out accusations against Holland. We have no proof. We *could*, after all, be wrong in our assumptions." He held up his hand against the obvious objections the girls were about to make. "I don't want Holland to know we are suspicious of him for two excellent reasons, Donna. First, it could put Bee in some danger. She was the one who actually saw him at the inn near the Gypsy wagon in which Sir Thomas was held captive. Number two, I would like him to think he is safe." Again he held up his hand for silence, as he could see they were about to interrupt him. "If he is a desperate man, and we still don't know for certain that he is, then he needs Thomas out of the way and means to carry on. However, he might be careless if he thinks no one is the wiser for this last escapade. What we need to do is keep Felix under watch while we have Sir Thomas under protection."

"That's the ticket!" Robby agreed. "How do you mean to do that?"

"The girls needn't worry their pretty little heads over such things Rob, but rest easy, it will be taken care of," his lordship answered.

"Well!" Bee said, putting her hands on her hips, "of all the paltry things. We rescued Thomas, after all, and I think we are entitled to be in on this to the end."

Again his lordship touched Bee's fair cheek. "Pretty little thing when she is angry, isn't she?"

Lady Bee glared and stamped her foot, but it was to no avail; his lordship would speak no more on the subject.

Two days had passed since young Sir Thomas had been returned to the Russells. Lady Bee was out walking in the evergreen garden with Lord Connwood and questioning him unmercifully.

"But, my lord—"

"John," he interrupted her. "I do think you should be calling me John."

She blushed. "I cannot."

His brow went up. "Why the deuce not?"

"I don't know," she answered simply. "Besides, don't change the subject." She peeped up at him adorably. "I don't understand why you can't tell me what you arranged with Mr. Russell for Thomas's protection. It is just that Papa will be coming for me in the morning, and I will be off for London and should rest easier knowing that—"

"That Thomas is in good hands? Don't you trust me, love? I have assured you that I have met with

Mr. Russell and made suitable arrangements for his protection. Is that not enough?"

She looked up at him and answered softly, "The wonder is that, yes, that is enough and, yes, I do trust you . . . completely. Could you not satisfy my curiosity, though?"

She had touched him with her sincerity and then captivated his sense of humor with her persistence. "Perhaps when I see you in London, I shall do so."

"Then you *are* coming to London!" She clapped her hands.

"Of course, monkey. What? Did you think I would miss your ball?" he answered with a laugh.

She blushed. "Oh . . . then you are only coming for the ball? That shan't be for another three weeks."

"Well, child, we shall see. I must stay to oversee the breeding of your father's mare next week."

"Yes." She sighed. "It was really too bad that we missed her season. When she arrived yesterday, I had so hoped we could breed her while I was still here."

"Never mind, brat. You shall have a glorious time in London gadding about with Donna and all the ton."

"I would rather stay here," she answered with a sigh.

He laughed. "Yes, I have grown all too used to your company. It is just as well that you are going."

"Well, of all the most horrible things to say." She had her hands on her hips.

He laughed robustly this time and took her face in his hands. "Forgive me, but it wouldn't do, you know."

"What wouldn't do?" she pursued.

"You, staying on here . . . I would forget myself," he answered on a low, soft note.

"Would you? I would like that," she answered quietly, her eyes looking full into his.

There was no resisting the impulse. He bent and brushed her lips gently with his own. Sparks of sensation shot through him, and he was caught up in sudden, overwhelming desire. He took her full into his arms, felt her supple, provocative body melt against him as his lips parted hers. Even as she pressed herself to him, gave herself to his kiss, he was pushing her away, saying all too harshly, "Go back to the house, Bee."

She ignored the roughness of his tone and snuggled into his arms. "But, my lord—"

"Go on!" It was nearly a shout. "Now."

She stood a moment and looked up at him in puzzlement. He could see the confusion in her bright eyes but restrained himself from assuaging it. She put out her hand to his chest. "But . . . ?"

"Don't you understand?" he cut her off on a cruel note. "I am not in the habit of seducing virgins, let alone one that is under my protection while her father is away."

She looked at him steadfastly. "Is it that . . . or is it that you are in love with someone else?"

He looked at her for a long moment. He had never spoken of Lady Sarah, but of course she might have heard rumors. Why had he never told her about Lady Sarah? There was no time to contemplate this question now, so he answered her gently, "No, I am not in love with someone else."

"Yet you mean to offer for the Lady Sarah?" Bee pushed boldly forward, needing to know.

He controlled himself from snapping at her. He reminded himself that this was his fault for leading the poor girl on, and then he tried to answer her honestly. "It is what I am expected to do."

"And so you shall?"

"And so I must," he answered on a hard note.

She did turn away then and move toward the house, forcing herself not to run, but she wanted to—oh, how she wanted to run.

Chapter Eighteen

The Earl of Saunders strutted his lovely daughter proudly on his arm. They had been in London for only three days, but already she was being hailed as a diamond of the first water. He was well liked by all the beau monde, and their house was constantly full of callers and invitations. The earl would have been much satisfied had he been able to find some measure of happiness in his daughter's eyes. Oh, she threw herself into the festivities with her usual bubbling style, but there was something there in her expression that betrayed her heart, and he frowned over the matter.

They were at a rout being given by the Lady Jersey, one of London's famous hostesses, and he stood back watching his daughter flirt outrageously with Beau Brummell. Donna was flitting by, and he caught her elbow. "Ho there, child, give me a moment, do," he said quietly.

Donna eyed him doubtfully. "What is it, my lord?"

"Bee. Tell me what is troubling her."

Donna sighed. "I can't. She would kill me and, in truth, you wouldn't want me to betray her. When she is ready, she will talk about it. Never mind—she'll do. She always does." Then Donna stopped, stared, and breathed, "Oh, no. Faith, there is Lady Sarah Grey!"

"And pray, what is that to say to anything?" the earl inquired almost roughly.

"I had better go to Bee." Donna was already moving toward her friend.

The earl stood back and contemplated this thoughtfully. Whatever was going on here? Why should Donna feel it necessary to run to Bee just because the Lady Sarah had arrived? What could it mean?

Someone at Lady Bee's elbow whispered to a friend, "Here is Lady Sarah. They say Connwood means to offer for her this month after she comes out of mourning."

"Never say so!" answered her companion. "I don't think they will deal—"

"Hmm. But what is that to say to anything? Their fortunes should deal famously." The other laughed.

Bee felt her heart cringe as she looked at the Lady Sarah and listened to these two women. Sarah was not an arresting figure. She was dressed in a deep violet half-mourning gown that did not suit her auburn locks. Her figure was full and her laugh high-pitched. Still, Bee had to allow that she was a pretty thing as she watched Sarah flirt with the young man at her side. Donna nudged her friend and said, "Come, Bee." She looked at Brummell. "I am going to steal Bee from you for a moment."

"Donna, you rogue!" The Beau laughed. "Just when I was finally enjoying myself." He bowed to Bee and took her hand. "I earnestly beg that you return to me as soon as this minx will allow."

Bee giggled, and Donna responded with a laugh. "I'll give her back to you when I am done."

"Just a moment here, don't I have anything to say about this?"

"Bee, hurry," Donna urged as she dragged her along the drawing room to stand behind two dowagers chatting forcefully. "Perfect," Donna breathed.

"What the—" Bee started impatiently and then realized Lady Sarah and her dashing male companion were just within earshot.

"Darling," the fair-haired gallant said, "can we not retire to the garden, where I might recite my latest verse to you?"

The Lady Sarah rapped his white-gloved knuckles with her brightly sequined fan and tittered. "Naughty boy . . . and what would people say? Besides, it is too cool an evening to stroll in the gardens." She eyed him coyly. "You may recite your verse to me here."

Donna and Bee exchanged wide-eyed stares as the man said softly, "Lady Sarah, fair and dear . . ."

"What the deuce are you two doing?" It was Sir George Fleetwood. At any other time his sudden appearance would have been a welcome occurrence. Now, Donna nearly growled at him as Bee pulled a face.

"Well," Sir George said, highly insulted, "I can see old friends are easily forgotten." So saying, he started to turn away.

Lady Bee yelped as she reached out and took hold of his arm. "Fleetie, don't be such a ninny!" Finding him responsive to this, she flung herself into his arms. "I am so pleased to see you again. When did you arrive in London?"

"That is better." He grinned and smoothed his wide lapels. "Got in only an hour ago. Changed, went right over to your place; your man said you had all come here." He smiled at Donna, who was waiting her turn. "Hallo, wild one," he said easily as she bent toward him and planted an amiable kiss upon his cheek. "You two been up to no good, I can tell."

"No, it isn't true. We have been angels ... heroines, in fact," Bee laughed. The next thirty minutes found the threesome deeply immersed in their conversation as Bee and Donna told about their adventure with Sir Thomas and the Gypsies. Robby joined them toward the end of their recital and assured Fleetwood—who had accused them of exaggeration—that they were indeed giving a fairly accurate account of their adventure. It was just about then that Felix Holland entered the room.

"Deuce take it if all the fish aren't out tonight," Donna breathed on a hushed note.

Her husband pulled a face at her. "I do wish you would watch your cant expressions, girl," he said, and then he spotted Holland and gave a low whistle, "What's to do now?"

"Remain calm. He doesn't know we suspect him," said Lady Bee, who nonchalantly gave Holland her back, with every indication that she had not seen his entrance.

"It won't fadge," Fleetwood said on a low note. "He is coming this way."

"Devil!" Bee breathed. "Oh, but I wish Connwood were here."

"Look," Donna put in, now in full panic, "we don't know anything. We just don't know anything. Understood?"

"For pity's sake!" snapped her husband, who was also nervous over the affair. "How can you say you don't know anything?"

"Because we don't, that's all. Can't question us if we don't know anything," Donna retorted defiantly.

"Stu-u-upid!" Bee elongated the word. "We, my girl, were the ones, if you recall, who found Sir Thomas and returned him to Mary Russell. How the deuce can we claim that we don't know anything?"

"I am not talking," Donna answered then. "I am just not going to talk. You answer him if you like. I know nothing. All I did was what you asked. I went with you to the camp, and I held the horses."

"Right," Bee returned with an accompanying look of disgust, "you say nothing."

"Well someone had better say something and soon," Fleetwood put in, "because—" He turned to Holland and said jovially, "*Felix*, how are you?"

Chapter Nineteen

Felix Holland rattled off amiable greetings to Lady Bee's little group. His eyes were intent as he leveled a look at Bee and said softly, "I understand that I have you and Mrs. Huxley to thank for the safe return of my little cousin, Thomas."

"Indeed, it was by the merest chance." Lady Bee smiled with cool disregard.

"Chance? How so?" Felix returned. "My cousin Mary tells me that you two knew that Thomas was being held by this Gypsy, went right into the camp, and rescued Thomas in bold fashion." He shook his head. "Astounding, when one contemplates the dangers involved."

"Ah, but you see" Fleetwood put in, "you know nothing of Mrs. Huxley and Lady Barbara. They are forever throwing themselves into the covert . . . usually among the first to sight the fox."

Felix eyed Fleetwood for a moment, looking for any hidden meaning. "Are they?" he returned cautiously.

"Hoydens." Robby said with a shake of his head. "Always been neck-or-nothing gals."

"Indeed," Felix said. "However, there is still the question of why *that* particular Gypsy wagon, that particular Gypsy camp?"

"Oh, didn't Mrs. Russell tell you the whole?" Bee asked in mock surprise and felt a moment's pride in her acting ability. "We were at the carnival, and I had a glimpse of a young boy's woebegone face at the window of a green wagon settled somewhat apart from the other wagons. It seemed odd to me, for he had such a fair face, such a bright shade of yellow hair. Well, he didn't appear to be of Gypsy descent. Then we met you and Mrs. Russell. She showed me the minature—remember?" Bee shrugged her shoulders. "Thought we would go and have a look."

He shook his head in some open disbelief. "Odd, that."

Donna could have pinched herself, for she hadn't meant to speak unless necessary, but she found herself frowning and asking Holland, "Why is that odd?"

"That you should assume Sir Thomas and the face of a young boy in a Gypsy wagon to be one and the same. That you should remember that face, immediately recognize it from a minature," Holland retorted, looking at Bee intently enough to make her cringe inwardly, "and that you should see the face of a boy at the window when that same boy was bound and lying in a corner of the wagon."

"How did you know that?" Bee asked softly.

"Oh, Thomas is full of praise. He recounted your daring rescue to me in some detail."

"Did he? But I did see his face at the window . . . and although he was bound when I found him, perhaps his legs were not always so?"

"Perhaps," Felix said.

Donna felt herself tremble.

Lady Bee knew at once that Felix had recalled seeing them at the inn the afternoon of the Stonehenge expedition. She looked at him now and smiled a half smile that conceded his point. What could he do? Nought. She spoke softly then, "I always play by instinct, Mr. Holland, and my instincts usually prove out."

"Ah, but instinct often leads us into danger," he answered with a warning in his voice.

"So it does, but forewarned is forearmed," Bee answered on a hard note.

He inclined his head and allowed her a cold smile. "Yes, indeed, but tell me if you will, when Mary had you look at the miniature of my young cousin, did you recognize him at once?"

She eyed him carefully and then decided to answer him. "At once."

"Yet you did not say so to Mary. Why is that?" He appeared casual in his manner.

"I did not want to raise false hopes," Bee returned easily.

"Of course," he answered, and there was no longer any doubt in his mind. Her meaning, her intent, was clear. Once again he inclined his head and politely took his leave. When he was out of earshot, Donna breathed out loud and remarked nervously, "Devil. He is a veritable devil and, Bee, I don't like it."

"Hmm," Fleetwood agreed. "Seemed to me the fellow has overstepped his mark. Came near to threatening you, damn it, Bee, did threaten you with both Robby and me standing by. Certes, the man is desperate. Only desperate men go that length." He shook his head. "Don't like it, either."

Bee pulled a face at him. "Don't be so melodramatic. He was warning us off, but it was an empty warning. All bark."

Robby had been thinking this over and suddenly announced, "Agree with Donna. He is a devil. Don't like it, either. Don't want him barking at you two.

112

Don't want him near either of you, either. Loose screw: no telling what he might do. You and Bee stay out of his way," he ended, wagging a finger at his wife.

"Sh, Robby, never mind," soothed his wife, who could see that his placid temper had been ruffled. A new fear gripped her, for he had the look of a man who meant to stand guard over her.

"Never mind?" he exclaimed in high-pitched tones. "Never mind? Ha! Mean to keep watch." So saying, he leveled a hard stare at Felix Holland's retreating form.

Donna and Bee exchanged amused glances, and Bee smiled as Donna took Robby's hand and coaxed, "Come on, Robby, I think they are serving refreshments now."

The following morning found Donna and Bee riding sedately in Hyde Park. It was a clear, crisp morning, but neither one was inclined to break the beau monde's rule of never galloping in the park, for they were totally absorbed with rehashing the events of the previous evening. However, they were soon distracted from this when Donna spotted Lady Sarah being guided to a park bench by the same gentleman they had seen her with at the evening's rout.

"Look!" Donna said in some excitement. "Ugh, whatever is she wearing on her head?"

Donna referred to the straw bonnet which was adorned with birds and flowers and not quite to Donna's more tailored taste.

"Never mind the hat. What about the beau? Isn't he the same fellow—and, Donna, look how he is kissing her wrist!" Bee answered her friend on an indignant note.

"Hmm, but there need be nothing in that, Bee.

After all, she is not in love with Connwood. It is an arranged marriage to unite two noble houses and their lands."

"Yes, but, Donna, she looks as if she rather likes that fellow," Bee objected.

"Hmm." Again Donna considered Lady Sarah and her attractive companion. "Perhaps she does. I suppose she means to carry on discreetly and still have her well-planned marriage."

"That is disgusting!" Lady Bee was outraged.

"Don't be such a green girl." Donna tittered. " 'Tis done all the time. It wouldn't suit you and it wouldn't suit me, but 'tis done all the same."

"Oh, Donna, I don't want that for"—she found she couldn't say his name—"him."

"No, 'tis a shame, for I rather think he has a tendre in your direction. Star-crossed. It appears as though the two of you are meant to be star-crossed."

"I won't accept that. I just won't. I can't immediately perceive what is to be done, but until they post the banns . . . until he formally asks for her hand, he is a free man, and there is still a chance."

"Don't count on it, missy." Donna returned skeptically.

Then all at once Lady Bee's expression changed and her eyes took on a shine. There, riding toward them on a great big bay gelding was Lord Connwood. She thought for a moment she couldn't breathe and wondered how she had managed to live through the last few days without seeing his handsome face.

His lordship saw the girls at once as he rode through the Hyde Park's serpentine bridle path, but it was Lady Bee's form his eyes focused on. Damn, but she looked a beauty, with her curls collected over one ear and her dark brown velvet top hat rakishly set on her well-shaped head. Her matching brown velvet riding habit was adorned with black frogging and fit her figure in a most alluring fashion. Her welcoming smile warmed him, and he thought that life would be a sad thing without Lady Bee's smile and bright eyes. As he approached the girls, he noticed Lady Sarah and her companion conversing amicably on the park bench and frowned. What to do?

"My lord," Bee said softly, and yet managed to convey the high degree of pleasure she was experiencing in finding him already in London. "I did not think you would be in London until the end of the week. How very wonderful."

He chuckled. "Wonderful, is it?" He greeted Donna and urged his horse onward, motioning for the girls to ride abreast as he left the serpentine and Lady Sarah at his back.

"No more wonderful, I think, than the time you must have been having in London." His lordship eyed Bee quizzically.

"My lord, there is no comparison. London has been insipid when compared to the days we spent at Searington with you," she exclaimed sincerely.

He laughed out loud. "Now that, my monkey, is a round tale!"

She beamed at him warmly, pleased with what she took as a form of endearment. " 'Tis not. It's true." She turned to Donna for confirmation. "Isn't it?"

"Mercy, I might be sick," Donna said in some amused disgust. "What about the Venetian breakfast we were at the other day and the rout last evening? Insipid?"

"Oh, well, they were very nice," Lady Bee admitted easily, "but nought to our time at Searington." She then changed the subject, for she could see Donna was about to point out specifics to debate

115

this. "My lord"—she drew his attention with her eyes—"how did that mare of ours do? Did the breeding go smoothly?"

"She was a diamond. Stood there for him, no fuss, no hitch. My man is watching her now, and we should know in a few weeks if she doesn't come into season." He smiled easily. "And that is why I am here sooner than I had expected."

"Hmm. Papa will be so pleased. Have you seen him?" Bee returned happily.

"I am on my way there right now. There is a shortcut from my place to yours, right through the park," he answered, waving to a passing acquaintance.

"Oh? Are you situated in Kensington, then?" Bee inquired casually.

He chuckled and reached over to tweak her nose. "Know the city already, do you?"

She blushed and laughed in Donna's direction. "We have been about—" She cut herself off at this point to put up a hand to Robby and Fleetwood, who were coming toward them.

Connwood watched Bee's open affection for Sir George Fleetwood and frowned over the problem. Theirs was an easy friendship, but he could see that Sir George could be led from there into something more. He did not see Lady Bee encourage Fleetwood to other realms, yet she did nothing to stop his flirting with her. What then? Ah, bah! Never mind, he told himself; in no time at all she would have scores of beaus knocking at her door. What then? Indeed, what then?

Chapter Twenty

Some clouds had come along to partly obscure the sun and the clear blue sky they had enjoyed during the morning, but these scudding puffs were hardly noticed as Lady Bee and Donna discovered the wonders of the Pantheon Bazaar.

Donna held a pink satin ribbon up for Bee's inspection and happily exclaimed, "This is it. Doesn't it just match the shade of that new morning gown I purchased yesterday?"

Lady Bee gave it her consideration and decided that it certainly did match, and at such a bargain as well, before excusing herself. "I shan't be long Donna—I just mean to go back to that booth with the laces, for I think I'll buy that Belgian lace, the one with the pearls." However, even as she made her way through the hubbub of shoppers, she heard her name called, and in some surprise, she turned, for she thought she knew the youthful voice,

"Lady Bee, Lady Bee," the youth called excitedly.

"Thomas!" Bee exclaimed as she discovered him in the crowd. "What in heaven's name are you doing here?" Then with a frown she added, "Are you alone?"

"Came to London with Aunt Mary . . . and here

is my cousin, John." Then, confidingly and with a touch of superiority, he said, "He is one year younger than I."

"Yes, but are you here at the Bazaar alone?" Bee smiled at John Russell, who smiled back at her and shuffled his feet.

"No, Mr. Tibbs is here"— Thomas looked around—"somewhere." Then he pulled a face. "He is always about . . . somewhere."

"Who is Mr. Tibbs?"

"He is our new tutor," young John Russell answered. "Don't like him, and he doesn't know any French or Latin."

"Hmm, and he isn't up on Greek mythology, but"—Thomas shrugged his shoulders—"Aunt Mary said Pudding Face, John's old tutor, had to go visit his sick mother, and Mr. Tibbs was all she could get on such short notice."

Bee felt a wave of uneasiness. "Who recommended Mr. Tibbs to your aunt, Thomas?"

Again he shrugged. "Don't know. Pudding Face left . . . and Mr. Tibbs showed up. John is afraid of him."

"Afraid of him? Why?" Bee asked with a frown.

Her question went unanswered, for Thomas cautioned, "Sh, here he comes."

Lady Bee looked up and across to find a stocky man whose dress denoted his status of tutor in complete contrast to his rough appearance. His hair, though neatly combed, was without style. His face displayed the remains of what Bee thought were more than scuffles, for one jagged scar across his cheek made her open her eyes wide. Then he spoke, and she was startled to find that his speech was nowhere near that of an educated man. Faith, she thought, he is a cockney!

" 'Allo, miss," he said, and tipped his wool cap to her. "Be ye a friend of the boys 'ere?"

"Tibbs," Thomas said, pulling a face, "this is Lady Barbara Saunders. She is one of the ladies I told you about that rescued me."

"Aye. Thought as much." Mr. Tibbs nodded, evidently approving.

"Thomas, I shall stop by with Mrs. Huxley one morning and pay your aunt a morning call. Please give her my regards," Bee said, taking this opportunity to look around for Donna, who she thought must be wondering where she was by now. She inclined her head at the boys' tutor. "Mr. Tibbs."

"What about me?" John asked, eyeing her rather worshipfully.

She laughed and touched his nose. "And good day to you, Mr. Russell. I shall see you all again very soon."

Thus taking her leave, she rushed back to Donna to give her the news. Donna was loath to tear her attention away from the china bric-a-brac of forest ponies she had found but raised a brow at Mr. Tibbs's description.

"Doesn't sound like your ordinary distinguished sort," Donna commented, and then mildly shrugged, "but I suppose for two wayward boys—"

"Yes, but, Donna, if I didn't know better, I would say he looked very much like a—oh, like what my father once called a 'cull,' a man of the streets who lives by his fists and his wits, you know."

"Can't be. Mrs. Russell wouldn't hire anyone like that to give lessons to her own son as well as her cousin. Doesn't make sense."

"Yet there it is. Donna, we once had a Bow Street runner—remember that time some years ago? He had come into the neighborhood looking for someone. Well, this fellow reminds me of him."

Donna's eyes got round with excitement. "A Bow Street runner? Faith, girl! What would a runner be doing with the Russells?"

"I don't know, but I tell you what," Bee said thoughtfully. "I'll wager my Lord Connwood knows!"

"There, there, there!" Donna gushed drawing her friend away from the crowd of young women they had been amicably conversing with for the last five minutes.

"What the deuce is wrong with you?" Lady Bee asked in some surprise as Donna dragged her behind a potted palm.

"Lady Sarah! There—with that fellow we are forever seeing her with. Bee, come, let's try and get closer and hear what they are talking about."

"Donna, that's terrible. Besides, we can't. I don't perceive a way."

For a reply Donna took her friend's elbow and steered her through a throng of fashionables in Lady Jersey's drawing room to where Sarah sat in deep conversation with the fair Dennis Maxwell. He was holding her gloved hand, putting it to his lips and uttering in anguished accents, "But I must have you. Speak to your father. . . ."

"Dennis, he won't give up a title. He won't give up Connwood's title and estates and vast fortune," she returned, similarly anguished.

"Well, but I am not without means, and my family's heritage dates back to the Norman times," Mr. Maxwell objected.

"Yes, but—oh, Dennis, what are we to do? Mama is looking our way," Lady Sarah said, hurriedly withdrawing her hand and then gasping, to look up and find Lord Connwood towering above her.

"Lady Sarah," he said softly, "how good it is to see you again."

She fluttered. "Indeed"—she gave her hand to him, watched as he placed a perfunctory kiss upon her fingertips—"it seems an age since I have seen you last."

Connwood looked from her to Dennis Maxwell, whom he was but briefly acquainted with, and gave the younger man a cool nod of greeting. While he was not in love with Lady Sarah, he rather thought she should not be flirting in this public fashion while they had an understanding. He was not, however, allowed time to consider this any further, for an interruption came at that moment. Donna burst forward suddenly with Lady Bee reluctantly at her rear.

"My lord! Why, how nice. We had not expected you tonight, and Robby has been saying that you were just what the evening needed. He will be so glad you have come."

Connwood nearly frowned at her. What the devil was she babbling about? However, he then saw Lady Bee looking dreadfully white and uncomfortable at Donna's back, and he smiled warmly at her.

"Donna, I shall attend to your husband presently." Then to Bee he said, "Hello, monkey. Enjoying yourself?" Without realizing it, he was moving toward her.

She managed a smile for him but couldn't speak. He had the uncontrollable urge to stroke her cheek and soothe away the troubled look from her eyes. He said gently, "Insipid evening, eh?"

She beamed at him then. "Not with you here." It was softly spoken, for his ears alone.

"Come, allow me to introduce you to Lady Sarah and Mr. Dennis Maxwell." He turned and said,

"Mrs. Donna Huxley, and Lady Barbara Saunders."

Maxwell then got to his feet and bowed, and it was to his credit that he rattled off some idle chatter to dispel the awkward sensation that had descended over the assembled group. Robby and Fleetwood appeared then with a boisterous greeting for Connwood. This took some minutes, during which Lady Sarah excused herself, saying that she rather thought she saw her cousin waving to her from across the room. She asked Maxwell to attend her as she touched Connwood's gloved hand and exclaimed that she did not wish to take him from his friends. He watched her back for a moment before he returned his attention to Robby and Fleetwood.

Lady Bee waited for the men's animated conversation to subside before she pulled at the sleeve of Connwood's black dress coat. "My lord," she called quietly.

He looked sideways at her and then at his sleeve before raising his brow. She put her gloved hand over her mouth and giggled. "Well, I need your attention."

"You do?" he asked in a teasing fashion. "And so you have, from the first day we met, needed my attention." And then he added affectionately, "It is a thing I could never deny *you*."

She blushed. "You are being outrageous, and now is not the time for that. I need an answer, for I am terribly concerned and worried."

He frowned. "You need an answer to what? No question has been put to me."

She wagged a finger at him. "Don't quibble. What I want to know is, *who* is Mr. Tibbs?"

"Ah," his lordship returned with mild unconcern.

"Ah?" Bee retorted, her dainty hands going to her hips and a light kindling her gray eyes.

He smiled. Such a beauty. Her bobbing curls caught the glimmer of light and tantalized, and her eyes moved him to reach for her chin. "Ah," he answered her again, "what more did you want?"

"An answer, my lord. Please. I . . . care for Thomas."

"What makes you think I know who Mr. Tibbs is?" He brushed away a fleck of something off his left shoulder.

She knew this was an art and refused to be put off. "My lord, don't play games with me. You know, I wasn't sure, but when you just said 'ah' to my question, then I was sure. Please. He does not look like a tutor. Is there a chance that Felix Holland has installed him there?"

Momentarily forgetting they were in company, he reached out for her shoulders, but immediately dropped his hands. "My dear, no. Rest easy on that score."

"Then what, my lord?" she persisted.

"I have told you to rest easy. Is that not enough?" His brow was up.

"Oh, no," she groaned, "here is Felix Holland and, faith, John"—she used Connwood's given name for the first time—"he is coming this way!"

She started off almost involuntarily but found his lordship's grip on her elbow, keeping her in place. She raised her face to Connwood's profile. Evidently he wanted this confrontation. She looked around for Donna, who had long since detached herself and found another set of friends. Robby and Fleetwood were not far away, and she watched them as they glanced at Holland and then at Connwood, a silent question in the air. Connwood gave no in-

123

dication by word or sign what he wished them to do, yet they knew he wanted them near. They stood their ground, though Robby whispered to Fleetwood, "Damned business, this. Wish the girls were well out of it."

"Aye." Fleetwood agreed.

Felix greeted Connwood quietly and turned to smile at Bee.

"Well," Holland said after a quick nod, "you are looking as lovely as ever, Lady Barbara. My little cousin is right; you are, I think, quite the most attractive woman in London."

"Oh, does Thomas say that?" Bee smiled. "Ah, but then he hasn't had the opportunity to meet too many other London ladies."

"How is the little fellow?" Robby put in, inching toward the party.

Felix raised a brow. "Do you know my cousin? I wasn't aware of that."

"Aye, had the pleasure of making his acquaintance while he was with the Russells in the country. Better place for him there. London is no place for young boys."

"Don't you think so?" Felix returned easily, his eyes flicking toward Lady Bee. "But I mean to take him about, show him the sights."

"Well, at least they are together—he and his cousin John, I mean," Bee said, looking full at Felix.

"Hmm, yes, but John may not always join us . . . for one reason or another," Felix answered.

Fiend, Bee thought. He is taunting me. "No? Why is that?"

"Ah, yes, for instance, tonight he came down with a dreadful tummy ache, and I am certain Mary will want to keep him resting at home tomorrow. I promised Thomas a treat, and there is no reason why Thomas should forego it," Felix answered blandly.

"And of course," Connwood put in suddenly, his eyes glinting like steel, "no harm can come to Thomas while he is in your company."

Felix turned his head around and met Connwood's stare. Here was a worthy enemy and one he did not wish to tangle with now or later. Evidently Connwood was aware that he was toying with Lady Barbara, and evidently Connwood would not allow this to go on. He inclined his head. "As you say, my lord, when he is in my company, he can come to no harm." So saying, he bowed himself off.

"Loose screw!" Robby said under his breath. "What did all that mean? Think the fellow isn't all there," he answered himself with a finger pointing to his head.

Connwood turned to Bee, who was trembling slightly. "That was for your benefit. You fouled his plans once, and he meant only to provoke you now, worry you, which I hope he has not done."

She looked hopefully at Connwood. "That was true, wasn't it, about no harm coming to Thomas when he is out with that awful man?"

"Yes, that is true. Now, I want you to forget about Holland and everything else and enjoy the remainder of the evening," Connwood said.

"Where are you going?" she asked, knowing somehow that he was leaving.

"I am sorry, love, I only stopped by tonight for a short while—and that was to see you." This last was wrenched from him.

She blushed. "Not true, and you are very naughty to say such things."

He laughed. "Yes, perhaps I am, but the thing is, monkey, when I say those things to *you*, I mean them."

A few minutes later he was gone, and though Bee laughed and mingled with her friends, all pleasure in the evening had faded with his departing form.

Chapter Twenty-One

"What have you in your head now?" Donna questioned as she climbed into the hired hack coach behind Bee and spread her fine blue skirts around herself. "If ever I had wanted your father to forbid us a treat, it was this one, but does he? No. 'Fine,' he says. 'Off you go,' he says."

"Donna, I sent a note around to the Russells this morning, requesting the pleasure of Thomas's company for an outing, but Mary Russell replied that he was already promised to Felix, who was taking him to St. John's Wood for a cricket match."

"Faith, Bee, never say you think Thomas will be in danger today?"

"No, not exactly, though it did occur to me that Felix might decide to be set upon by highwaymen, during which time anything could happen to Thomas—and St. John's Wood, well . . ."

"Oh, no, oh, no. Shouldn't we have asked Robby and Fleetwood to accompany us?"

"They had already left for the morning. What, should I have bothered them at their club? Just on a suspicion? No. We will just go and bump into Holland and perhaps warn him off for the time being."

"Oh, God," Donna groaned.

They had arrived at the cricket grounds to find quite a throng gathering for the match, when Donna exclaimed in some surprise, "Bee . . . Bee, I don't believe it—the match is set for women! Look here at what it says." She moved close to the poster to read, " 'An elegant variation awaits us today, as eleven females of Surrey shall meet against eleven females of Hampshire.' " Donna turned to Bee. "Imagine that. I wonder if we shall like the game."

"Never mind the game; we don't have time for that. We have to find Thomas and Felix in this crowd," Bee said, pulling a face. She thought this was not going to be easy. Then Donna was pulling at her sleeve again.

"Bee, Bee, look—I can't believe it! The Lady Sarah, with only her maid in attendance. Faith, for a lady in mourning she manages to get around a bit, doesn't she?" Donna's brow was cocked.

Bee was momentarily diverted from her purpose and studied the Lady Sarah. "What in thunder is that woman doing here? Donna, tell me, is she here to meet what's-his-name?"

"Maxwell? Dennis Maxwell?" Again Donna's chin was pointing. "My my. Now, this is something that goes beyond heavy flirting. I was inclined to say, let the girl enjoy her amusements—Connwood certainly does—but this, this is something more, isn't it?" Donna was frowning.

"What do you mean, Connwood certainly does?" Bee turned on her friend, her eyes lightinng up militantly.

Donna laughed in response to this. "Bee, for goodness' sake, Connwood flirts everywhere he goes—you have seen him yourself—and with you he has taken on more than just a flirtation."

"Donna!" Bee objected.

"Donna? What do you mean, Donna? Admit it,

Connwood has displayed a marked degree of attention in your direction, and I believe that he is more than half in love with you."

Bee looked away. "You are absurd."

"Am I? Well, I don't think so, and what is more, the Lady Sarah is in love with that Maxwell character of hers, so it is very annoying that all of you are being robbed of happiness because no one will speak up."

"What do you suggest, then?" Bee demanded in some irritation.

Donna bit her lip. "I don't know, but I mean to walk over to the Lady Sarah and, er, pay my respects." She looked over her shoulder as she started off. "Are you coming?"

Bee wanted to hide, but she rather thought the best thing to do was to tag along with Donna on this one. Perhaps it would serve in some obscure way, though she didn't see how.

Lady Sarah's maid had melted into the crowd as Dennis had taken up his beloved's hand and started for a quiet bench away from the throng. Her ladyship was therefore quite horrified when she heard her name blasted on the air, for Donna had made sure her voice would carry.

"Sarah! Why, Lady Sarah!" Donna called cheerfully as she and Lady Bee approached. "How delightful to find you here. Lady Barbara and I thought we were the only ones who enjoyed a good cricket match." She paused and gave Mr. Maxwell her outstretched hand. "Dennis Maxwell, isn't it? Yes, of course, you are often together, you two, aren't you?" There was a tease in her voice as Dennis bent to drop a perfunctory kiss upon her gloved fingers.

"Mrs. Huxley," he responded politely.

"Yes, yes, Dennis and I are such old friends . . .

and Papa does not approve of ladies at sporting events, but I do so love cricket that . . . that Dennis offered to escort me," Lady Sarah said.

"To see the ladies play. Hmm. This should prove an interesting game," Donna replied.

"Ladies? What ladies?" Lady Sarah could not stop the question but knew as soon as it was out that she had been caught.

"Oh, didn't you know?" Donna pursued unmercifully. "If one followed cricket, one would know—it is posted everywhere on the grounds. But then, if one were here for other reasons—" Donna tittered effectively.

"Mrs. Huxley," Lady Sarah breathed, "please. I know that you and your husband are very close to Lord Connwood—"

"Indeed we are," Donna said, suddenly eyeing the woman coldly.

Lady Sarah's chin went up. "Ah, so you are. Well then, do your worst, Mrs. Huxley, do your worst. In the end I mean to have exactly what I want in all corners; mark me, for I always get my way." So saying, she boldly took Mr. Maxwell's arm and led him away.

Bee had been feeling guilty and sorry that they had attacked Lady Sarah, but on this last, her mouth opened in some surprise, and she turned to Donna. "I don't believe her. How dare she say such a thing? Doesn't she think you will take it back to Connwood?"

"She means to brazen it out," Donna replied, "but she is a fool. He may stick to tradition, but he won't allow her to publicly parade her indiscretions."

"They are not engaged to be married yet." Bee said, biting her lip. "She could say so to him. He has no real rights . . . not yet."

"Yes he does, in his mind," Donna returned,

"So be it. She doesn't understand the caliber of the man she is dealing with."

"I don't want him hurt, Donna. We must not tell him about this encounter," Bee said quietly.

"What?" Donna turned on her friend and took her shoulders. "This is what we need. I mean to quote the Lady Sarah to Connwood . . . and not miss a word."

"No. I won't have him hurt."

"He doesn't love her. He won't be hurt," Donna objected.

"His pride will be hurt, especially because we were involved." Bee said. "The matter is closed."

Donna sighed. "Right—but then what?"

"Perhaps he will find a way," Bee said. "Now, we came to find Felix and Thomas!"

"Hmm, but I have been looking, Bee, and they are nowhere about."

Bee felt deflated. "Well, let's walk about, then, and have a better look."

Chapter Twenty-Two

A warm spring sun beamed into the morning room of the Saunderses' town house. Donna sat sipping a cup of hot chocolate and restlessly perusing a gothic novel. She sighed and put it down for the tenth time in twenty minutes.

"Bee, should we perhaps go to the Russells' and make certain Thomas took no harm yesterday?" she asked.

The girls had never found Felix and Thomas at the cricket match the day before. Bee shook her head. "No, if there had been a problem, we would have heard by now." She got up and took to pacing.

"Bee, for pity's sake, stop that," Donna complained.

"It isn't only me," Bee returned, putting a hand to her well-shaped hip. "You feel it, too. I sense it."

Donna eyed her friend and pulled a face of disgust. "Yes, I do, but"—she shrugged—"what's to do? I wish Robby hadn't taken Fleetwood with him."

Bee frowned. "Why?"

"Then Fleetwood could have escorted us to the balloon ascension." She got to her feet and stretched daintily. "It is most provoking that your father is not here, either." Then a notion struck her. "Bee . . . ?"

"What?" Bee stood back from her warily.

"Why don't we send a note around to Connwood? He would take us," Donna returned gleefully.

"Donna!" Bee was momentarily shocked. "We couldn't." Then, as the idea took hold, she licked her bottom lip thoughtfully. "Well, not so boldly . . ."

There was no time to further contemplate this plan, for his lordship took it into his own hands by arriving at that moment. The Saunderses' butler appeared, and as he was announcing his lordship, Connwood strode through the open double doors. His eyes found Bee at once and softened. She was a beauty, with her curls collected over one ear and her form-fitting morning gown of blue displaying her curvacious charms. She clapped her hands together and immediately drew his laughter.

"My lord," Bee exclaimed, going to him and taking both his gloved hands in an unconscious welcome, "we were just this minute talking about you."

He looked to Donna and raised his eyes heavenward. "Then I should have followed my first instinct, which was to have my man drive past. What do you two lovelies want?"

Bee pouted and dropped his hands. He felt the loss, and without realizing how pointed his action was, he retrieved her fingers and held them. "No, no, monkey—tell me, do."

She smiled then and allowed him to go on holding her fingers.

"Would you be so kind as to take us to the balloon ascension? Papa expressively forbade us the treat without escort . . . and Robby took Fleetwood to Hampstead for the day on some business or other."

"Ah, so I am an afterthought," he said on a mocking note of melancholy.

Once more she withdrew her hands and her eyes looked away. "Never an afterthought."

He took her chin between his forefinger and thumb. "Bee, it would afford me the greatest pleasure on earth to be able to lend my escort to you and Donna. I came here with no other purpose than to ask you if you wished to come for a drive, and my open carriage awaits you outside."

Donna watched these two, and a sure dawning came over her. This was no longer a game. Lord Connwood was as much in earnest as Lady Bee. Faith! He was in love with Bee. Well, that settles the matter right and tight, she decided on the spot. Something must be done!

The vast green lawns of Hyde Park were covered with booths. People were mingling, smoking, drinking, in a fever of excitement for the Spring Fair was well on its way. His lordship purchased a basket of nuts for the girls as they wandered through the park toward the clearing, where Sadler's balloon was scheduled to ascend.

Bee found a fiddler, who winked at her as she passed, and she arched a shoulder at him for his lively tune. Connwood cocked a brow at her. "Too sassy by far," he said softly into her ear.

"Yes, he was," she answered with a giggle.

"I was talking of you, my girl."

"Yes, I know." She giggled again and would have skipped away from him had he not had the foresight to engage her hand and hold her near.

"Famous!" Donna remarked excitedly. "I cannot believe how fast they erected all this."

"Indeed, but I must say I wish they had not," his lordship returned. "Why the serenity of the finest park in London should be blasphemed with the stench of bad liquor and dirty people . . ." He was shaking his head over the matter as Bee cut in with her musical laughter.

"Grump. 'Tis only for a short while, after all."

"Aye, so they said back in '14. Certes, when I think of what they did then," he answered with a rueful smile.

"Hmm. Papa once mentioned it. Said the Prince Regent turned the park upside down. Everywhere you looked there were tents selling tobacco, liquor, cigars. He said it was dreadful."

"So it was. They filled the Serpentine with these ugly little things playing at war with their ridiculous ships . . . and rockets blasting all night. It was a horror, Bee. There wasn't a blade of grass to be seen, for it was covered with people and debris."

Donna said in defense of this, "Yes, but they were celebrating the end of Napoleon, for goodness' sake."

"Look, there—" Bee cut in quickly, before his lordship could retort irritably to this. "Isn't it wonderful?"

As they peered toward the large bright balloon being readied for ascension, a voice was heard at their backs. "Lady Bee . . . Lady Bee!"

Bee turned to find Sir Thomas and his older cousin, Felix Holland, coming toward them. In spite of herself she felt a shiver rush up her spine.

"Thomas, how splendid to find you here," Bee called brightly and held her arms out to him.

He gave her a bear hug and was called to order by his cousin. "Now don't crush the lady, Thomas." Felix managed a smile to soften the words.

"Sorry." Thomas said sheepishly, "It's going to go up." He referred to the balloon, and his face was full of his anticipation of this event.

"I certainly hope so." Bee laughed.

"Poor John . . . he couldn't come. Got sick. I think

it was the chocolates. Ate the whole box, nearly." Thomas returned.

Bee looked at Felix, who returned her look with a mocking smile and said for her ears alone, "Acquit me. I had nought to do with that, though it was an excellent notion."

She gasped. She couldn't imagine he would dare to speak in such a vein, and she looked at his lordship, who gave no indication of having heard this last. She managed to say, "Now, Mr. Holland, why should I think such a thing?"

"Why, indeed, yet I rather thought the idea came into your head." Again, so softly spoken, and this time with a lining of something she could not name. Was there a warning there?

"Have some nuts, Thomas," Donna said, holding the basket out to him, for she wanted him away from Holland. She could see that Connwood wished private conversation with Holland. "Come with me, and we'll have a closer look at that balloon of Sadler's, for I think 'tis the best I've seen yet."

"Aye," Thomas agreed, taking the basket she offered and falling into step beside her.

"Holland, what a good cousin you are to bring young Thomas here for a treat," Connwood said quietly.

"Yes, I rather think so," Holland returned, eyeing his lordship warily.

"Of course the fact that you are his heir has nought to do with it?" Connwood asked casually.

Holland's eyes snapped. "Now, how the devil did you find out I was his heir? It is not much known."

"So I was given to understand. However, Augusta Penistone is an old friend. She was good enough to tell me that her brother had a fear of the estates' not being carried on in the family name.

He altered his will to read that in the event of Thomas's death his fortune and his estates all go to the next male heir carrying the Holland name. That would be you."

Bee watched Holland in silence, for she could see his temper had been badly ruffled. "I was not aware that Augusta even knew about that. My uncle told me that I was next in line, not his sister, but I was led to believe that she would not be told."

"He made certain that she knew and did not resent his new will. She did not. She was well provided for by her late husband. She is, however, concerned for Thomas. She believes you are in dire straits, you see."

"Perhaps that is true, perhaps it is not, nevertheless, I cannot be responsible for Thomas when he is not within my protection," Holland answered. "What people think they know and what they can prove are often two very different items."

"Holland, be certain, if there is something *I* think I know, I shall most assuredly prove it."

"Thank you, my lord, for the warning. I shall keep it in mind," Holland said, tipping his top hat at Lady Bee and moving off to collect his young cousin.

Lady Bee turned to speak to Connwood and gasped, for moving behind some well-laid-out shrubbery was yet another familiar figure; it was Mr. Tibbs, the "tutor"!

"John . . . John, it is Tibbs there. I am sure of it. Oh, drat, he is out of sight, but, John, I saw him."

"Did you, love? Never mind. You said my name again and quite beautifully. I do so like to hear it on your lips."

She looked up into his eyes, but as she did so, she caught sight of yet another familiar figure. It was the Lady Sarah. She waited, but instead of coming toward them—and Bee was certain Sarah had seen them—the woman turned and nearly fled in the opposite direction, her maid hurriedly trying to keep step. Bee frowned and looked at his lordship, sensing from his expression that he had seen this as well.

Some moments later they rejoined Donna near the balloon site and caught a fleeting glimpse of Lady Sarah and Dennis Maxwell. Bee's sharp eyes met Donna's and cautioned her to silence, but Donna disobeyed her friend's silent command and exclaimed, "My lord, is that not your Lady Sarah— over there—with that Maxwell chap?"

"Indeed, Donna, you know very well that it is."

"Shall I wave to her?" Donna persisted.

"Do, and I shall wring your pretty neck." Lord Connwood smiled, not in the least perturbed.

Donna turned and beamed at Lady Bee, saying softly into her ear, "Now, if we can put this to use . . . ?"

Chapter Twenty-Three

Some days had passed since the morning they had met Sir Thomas in Hyde Park with Felix. Bee was sipping her morning coffee and idly perusing a fashion plate while Donna bade her husband a pleasant morning. He was off with Fleetwood and Connwood to see a boxing match. Donna turned and cocked her head and eyed her friend appraisingly.

"Well, what are you hatching in that zany brain of yours this morning?"

"I was just thinking that it is time we called on Mary Russell and looked in on Thomas," Bee said, getting to her feet and smoothing the skirt of her pale pink morning gown.

Donna pulled a face but in answer to this said, "Right, you go up and get our spencers, I'll have the carriage brought round."

Bee smiled. "It is such a nice day, we could walk. After all, they are not so far off."

"We'll go in the carriage," Donna said, looking down at her friend in a commanding fashion.

Bee laughed and agreed to this as she left the room and made for the stairs. Something was bothering her, but she couldn't quite get a grip on it. Some instinct moved her, and it was in Thomas's direction. Faith, she thought as a shiver rushed through her, whatever could be wrong? Nought. We would have heard if something were wrong. . . .

"Well, Mary, do hurry up," Felix urged. "We can stop and pick up your gown for the Saunderses' ball and stop by the chemist on our return if you like."

"Hmm, but with poor John ill upstairs, I do so dislike leaving Thomas on his own."

"Well then, Mr. Tibbs can keep the boy company if their lessons are over for the morning." Felix had her arm.

She laughed and admonished him, "Fine, but do wait till I have my cloak secured. I don't understand what the rush is all about anyway."

"Ah, the rush is that I should like to discharge these errands with you and still get to Weston's for my appointment later this afternoon. He is making me a new waistcoat for Lady Barbara's ball."

Mr. Tibbs appeared in the hallway at that moment, and Mary Russell cringed inwardly. Why her husband had insisted on hiring such a creature she could not guess, but she always adhered to Mr. Russell's decisions in such matters.

"Mrs. Russell." Mr. Tibbs inclined his uncovered head toward the lady of the house, and then said, "Mr. Holland."

"Ah, Tibbs, there you are. I shall be going out with Mr. Holland. Perhaps it would be best if you were to keep Sir Thomas company until my return."

"Aye. He be abovestairs playing at cards with young John, but I'll be nearby, don't ye fret."

"Er, no, I shall try not to," Mrs. Russell said with a frown as she turned and gave her hand to Mr. Holland's waiting arm.

They had not been gone more than five minutes when the Russell butler opened the door, to find a small and filthy urchin standing before him,

"Eh, covey, Oi got this 'ere important note for Sir Thomas. Oi'm to give it to nobbut 'im. Oi'm promised another coin when Oi does."

The Russell butler was inclined to send the boy about his business. However, the lad waved the sealed note before his eyes and added, "Better let me do me job, or they might be trouble, ye know."

There was no saying but the dirty urchin might be right. Well, there was no harm in it after all. The boy was only delivering a note and then would be on his way. He advised the lad to follow him upstairs and not to dare stray from his back.

Thomas looked at the boy and then at the note, saying out loud, "Zounds, John, who could that be from?"

"Well, take it. Let's see."

At this Thomas dug in his pocket for a coin and gave it to the urchin, who was then led away by the butler. "Right, then, let's see," Thomas said in some excitement.

Dear Sir Thomas:

I was very impressed with you when your cousin introduced us yesterday before my balloon ascension.

You expressed a wish to take a flight in the balloon with me, and I have decided to allow you this treat this very afternoon.

If you will meet me at the Three Bulls Tavern in Soho, we can proceed together to Green Park, where my balloon awaits.

You will no doubt wish some privacy, as your guardians might forbid the expedition to you. Do come alone.

> Very truly and obediently yours,
> Eric Sadler

"Zounds, John, zounds!" Thomas exclaimed in a fever of sudden excitement. "Swear you won't tell!"

"I swear it," John replied at once. "What—what?"

"I am going up in a balloon. Today. I must escape Tibbs."

"A balloon? No! Yes, I mean—but Mama won't like it." John seemed troubled over this. "Do you think you should?"

"Pooh!" Thomas returned. "What? Am I a baby in shortcoats?"

"Well, not much older, and I am sure Papa won't like it, either," John answered.

"I shall take the back stairs. Wish me luck, John."

"Aye and myself, for I will be the one they go after when you aren't here," John groaned, pulling the covers up to his neck.

"They can't do anything to you. You are sick." Thomas laughed on his way out of the room.

The Saunderses' coach pulled up along the curbing outside the Russells' leased London lodgings, but even as the postilion opened the door for Lady Barbara to alight, she caught sight of Thomas running across the street.

"Thomas!" Bee called, and had the felicity of seeing him turn and then hurry off. "Well," she exclaimed, and then something, she didn't know what, made her start after him, calling to Donna, "Follow me as best you can with the coach, Donna. I'm off to see what that boy is up to!"

Donna leaned out of the coach in some concern. "Bee—Bee, you can't . . ." Then to herself she added, for her friend already was hurrying away, "There she goes, running through the streets of London like a perfect hoyden, with her ball only a few days away . . . and what is to be done?" She answered herself and called to her driver, "After your mistress if you can!"

Thomas had run off from the house at an exceptional pace, but satisfied that he was out of range, he glanced behind, did not see Lady Bee, who had ducked into a doorway, and then proceeded at a less heady speed. Still, Lady Bee found herself striding hard in order to keep him in sight. It was when she saw him dodge into an alleyway that she really began to worry and took actually to running, for now she meant not only to keep him in sight but to catch him up.

Thomas bought her some time when he stopped to ask directions to the Three Bulls Tavern. However, just as she was about to gain some distance, a coach and four came barreling across the street and into her path. She was obliged to wait until this had passed before she could see Thomas, still heading toward London's Soho district. Five minutes later he was no more than fifty feet in front of her. Bee thought her legs would give way and her lungs would burst, when he suddenly turned, saw her, and, with his eyes opened wide, stood stock-still.

"Lady Bee . . ." he breathed out loud as she moved toward him.

"Thomas . . . Thomas, where do you think you are going?" she managed to ask on a breathless note.

"You followed me," he accused.

"Yes, I did. Are you angry?" she returned, attempting meekness all at once.

He eyed her from a half-shaded gaze and considered this. "Well, it is wrong to follow a friend."

"Yes, you are right, but I was dreadfully worried about you," she answered.

"Yes, well, I am fine, so you may go home now," he answered.

"Can't," she returned blandly.

"Why not?" he asked in some surprise.

"Don't know how. Lost. I was never in this part of London, and I don't think I should really travel back myself—without an escort—do you?"

Here was the rub. Thomas knew his duty as a gentleman. He was only a boy, but even if this weren't the very lady who had rescued him, even if she weren't the lady whom he adored, he still could not throw her to the wolves. It had occurred to him that he might be nearing the Three Bulls Tavern, but it was bringing him into a terrible section of London.

"Aye," he grunted, "can't let you go alone." Then he sighed. "Now, what shall I do?"

"What were you bound to do? Where were you going?" she asked gently.

"Secret?" He eyed her suspiciously. She was a girl. She wasn't bound by the same codes.

"Right then, a secret," she answered promptly, not at all bound and hoping he wouldn't realize this.

"Got a letter from Sadler . . . said he would take me up in his balloon if I would meet him at the Three Bulls Tavern. Said I should come alone."

"Alone? Take you up in his balloon? I don't believe it," she answered in some amazement.

He eyed her for a moment and gave this a thought. "Well, it has been bothering me. Yesterday, when Felix brought me to meet him and I asked if I could go up with him, he said no, wouldn't even discuss it. Then he invites me up. Odd, that." He shrugged. "But I'm not about to turn him down."

"Thomas, I have a bad feeling about this," Bee said, suddenly more frightened than she had been a moment ago. The Three Bulls Tavern was directly across the street, and it had a filthy, evil look about it. "Let's go home." She looked around for Donna and her coach, but evidently they had not been able to keep her in sight. Right, then, here they were in one of the worst spots in London with all sorts sidling by them.

"And miss my chance at a ride in a balloon?" Thomas shook his head. "You wait here Lady Bee. You needn't come into that tavern; it doesn't look the sort of place a lady should enter. I'll go and fetch Mr. Sadler, and we'll all leave together. How is that?"

"I am coming with you," Bee said staunchly.

Thomas shrugged but took her hand. "Right, then, stay close to me."

She smiled to herself but only briefly, for just then they passed a tall, burly man in dirty clothes, who looked her over thoroughly and advised her that he thought her "prime, jest prime."

Chapter Twenty-Four

"Well now, look at this twig of a boy," said a stout man dressed in dark wools who came up alongside of Thomas. "Ye must be the little Sir Thomas who wants to go up in the balloon."

"Who are you?" Thomas asked, making something of a face of disgust.

"Oi be the man who will be toiking ye to the balloon—if yer a good lad and don't give me no trouble, that is."

"I don't think so," Lady Barbara said firmly. "Come, Thomas, I think we will go home now."

Thomas had his doubts. The more time that went by the more doubts he had. Suddenly they were confirmed. This was not Eric Sadler, and this was not the sort of person Eric Sadler would consort with. Something was very wrong. "That's right," Thomas answered, and looked defiantly at the man. "I've decided not to go up in the balloon today." He took Lady Barbara's hand. "Come along, Lady Bee," he said, playing the young gentleman.

"Not so fast, my little covey," the man said. "Been paid to bring ye along, and bring ye along Oi mean to do. Jack Wold always gives whot he is paid to give." He looked at Lady Bee. "Ye be, on the other hand, not quite paid for, but then, can't be

146

letting you go running off bringing down the runners on me 'ead, now can Oi?"

"You can't really stop me, can you?" Bee said, making for the door. She looked at Thomas. "Now, Thomas, let's leave."

"I can't, Lady Bee," the boy said on a worried note.

Lady Barbara looked at the man called Jack Wold. He was smiling and displaying a set of yellow broken teeth, but he had Thomas's shoulder in hand. In his other hand he held a glinting knife, and it was poking Thomas nicely in the back.

"Ye'll both be coming with me. Oi 'ave me vehicle"—he elongated the word—"waiting ye in the back."

Donna and the Saunderses' coach were unable to keep up with Lady Bee and Thomas. Their quarry was very soon hopelessly lost to them. Donna stopped the coach and nearly cried with vexation, and then she spotted Lord Connwood on his bay gelding.

"My lord—John!" she called, her voice filled with her anxiety.

Connwood heard his name and looked to see the Saunderses' coach, with Donna hanging out the window. He shook his head, and as he managed to wield his horse through the traffic to her side, he teased, "Will you never cease being a hoyden?"

"My lord," Donna breathed, ignoring this last for the moment, "there is something wrong. Bee saw Thomas running off and went after him. When we last saw them, they were pointed towards Soho!"

"What the devil?" He frowned. "Where are they now?"

"That is just it. I don't know—and there is something about all of this that frightens me. What should we do?"

"Let's go back to the Russell place and see what they know," Connwood said, making a split moment decision.

It wasn't much later that both Donna and Connwood were in the sickroom questioning John Russell, who begged off in a frantic way,

"Can't tell you anything, don't you see? It's a secret. Gave my word of honor," John said. "You understand that."

"Yes, I do," Connwood said, thinking this over.

"Well, I don't. Here is your best friend, your cousin, perhaps in danger, and all you are worried about is your honor!" Donna turned to Connwood. "Talk to him."

"He is perfectly right. He gave his word; it is his bond." He looked young John over, and he could see the boy was worried. He would try another tactic. "You know, however, that your word need not be broken."

"How?"

"Well, perhaps something happened which you did not pledge a secret. Something that might help us find Thomas on our own without your help."

John's eyes lit up. "Yes, yes—he got a note, that is not a secret, though I can't tell you who it was from."

"Right, John. Where is that note now?" Connwood pursued.

"Here, here in my wastebasket," John cried happily, and then added, "But it isn't right to read another man's mail, you know."

"No, it isn't right, except in extreme cases, like now, where I believe it is a matter of life and death."

"Is it?" John's was a small voice.

Connwood smiled reassuringly. "Perhaps not." He fetched the note, opened it wide, and smoothed it over before reading it out loud to Donna, who was impatiently waiting.

"Three Bulls Tavern is one of the worst dives in all of London," he breathed, and then said to John, "Where is Tibbs?"

"Thomas meant to duck him," John answered.

"Thank you, lad. We'll bring your cousin home safe and sound, see if we don't," Connwood said, taking Donna's elbow and leading her out of the room.

A quick survey told them that Tibbs was nowhere to be found, and as they moved outdoors, Donna insisted on knowing the answer to Bee's never-ending question, "Who is Tibbs?"

"Mr. Russell and I hired a Bow Street runner to watch over Thomas. That is who Mr. Tibbs is, and much good it has done us." Connwood growled.

"For goodness' sake. Bee was right," Donna returned, wide-eyed.

"Donna, go home. Robby and Fleetwood should be there by now, or will be soon. Send them to meet me at the Three Bulls Tavern in Soho."

"Yes, but I want to go with you." She pouted.

"It is no place for a lady, and I don't want to worry about you. Just do as I say. I don't have time to argue." He was already mounting his horse, which had been walked by a lackey for the brace of a coin.

Donna watched him ride off and sighed. Well, she had better hurry and fetch Robby, but it wasn't fair that Robby would get to be on this last adventure while she sat home, she thought, pulling a face as she advised the Saunderses' driver to return her to Saunders Place.

Chapter Twenty-Five

"I could scream," Lady Bee offered, attempting to reason with Jack Wold.

"Aye, that ye could, Miss Fancy Piece, but who would 'elp ye 'ere?"

"Oh, I don't know . . . There might be one gentleman in this place."

He grunted out a short laugh. "Go on, then, scream. See 'ow many come running."

Lady Bee looked around and then boldly, lustily, let go a scream to wake up the dead. Some heads turned in her direction; one man even held a tankard of beer up to her and grinned, but no one was roused enough to move in her direction, let alone come to the rescue. Jack Wold chuckled. "Good. Now that ye got that out of yer system, we best be going, for Oi don't want to 'arm this lad if Oi don't 'ave to. But Oi will if ye put up any struggle, Oi'll run 'im through on the spot, make no mistake, missy—Oi'll do it." His voice took on a grimness that made Bee fully aware he did indeed meant what he said. Quietly she allowed him to push her through the galley, through the back room, to a door that opened into a dark alleyway. There another grizzled, round, short man stood beside a rackety old carriage,

"Who be the mort, Jack?"

"Just another mort, don't matter to me, don't matter to you. She'll 'ave to go with the young flash," Jack Wold answered, shoving Bee roughly into the carriage.

"Oi don't loike it," the short, round man announced. "We wasn't paid fer two. This rig called for the boy."

"Stop yer blabbing, ye curst fool. Think Oi want the mort on me 'ands? Oi don't hold wit that, but was Oi to let her go screaming to the runners? She came along, and now she be in it—nought Oi can do about that."

"Yeah, well Oi don't loike it," Wold's accomplice repeated. "Aw, jest shake yer shambles, and let's be off," Wold said in some disgust as he threw Thomas within the carriage and secured that door shut.

Lady Bee, within, had already tried the door on her left and found it shut tight against escape. There was nothing for it but to hope for some means of escape during the journey these two meant to accomplish with them.

"Don't be scared, Lady Bee," Thomas whispered and felt himself trembling.

"Now, why would I be frightened, my buck? I have you with me, and there is Donna, who no doubt followed me to the tavern and is even now getting us help." She put her arm around Thomas and held him to her.

"It's all my fault," Thomas sniffed.

"Now, isn't that a foolish thing to say? Fault, indeed! If there is a fault, 'tis fate's, not yours or mine, and I tell you for certain, Thomas, fate has always been on my side and is still, I think, so don't you worry, we'll do."

He smiled at her, but then he frowned as he

looked out the small carriage window and found Wold closing its shutter. "Famous!" Thomas muttered. "We won't even be able to see what direction he takes us."

"No, we won't, but we will be able to listen, and our hands are still free," Bee said, more to herself than to him. Indeed, she had to think of something she could do, but what? Just what?

"Well and damn!" Robby exclaimed as he and Fleetwood raced their horses as fast as they dared through the busy London streets.

"Aye, this is a rare kick-up, and what it all means, I daren't think about."

"Means?" Robby asked. "What should it mean? That poor lad has no doubt run into trouble, and Bee must be right there in the thick of it. Have you a barking iron?"

"Aye, took it to the match with us this morning. Those things tend to get a bit resty and . . . well, so we have one between us now."

"Good man!" Robby was pleased. "It's a thousand pities I don't have mine. I should like to put a hole through that Felix fellow. My little Donna was near to tears with worry."

Fleetwood smiled to himself, for Donna was a tall Juno of a lovely that he would never have thought of as "little," but as Robby said, she had been quite hysterical when she had recounted what had happened. "Don't like this," Fleetwood said with a dark frown as the directions they had obtained brought them into London's worst section. "To think that young rascal and Bee came here on foot . . ."

"Aye," Robby agreed grimly. "Look there—*Connwood!*"

Connwood spotted them nearly in the same moment and moved his horse across the avenue. "I have already inquired within." He nodded toward the tavern down the road. "Lady Bee was certainly seen, but no one would say anything more."

"What then?" Robby asked.

Connwood was looking harried. "I am momentarily at a loss. It is my belief that they must have been taken in a closed coach."

"What avenue lies behind the tavern?" Fleetwood asked thoughtfully.

"Damn! Of course . . ." Connwood said, already moving off. They found the alleyway, and as they took its length, Connwood stopped a street urchin and inquired if the boy had seen a closed coach come through.

"Aye, that Oi did, guv," the boy said, and held out his hand.

His lordship flipped a coin into the dirt-covered hand. "Right, then, which way, lad?"

"Took Booth Road, it did. Funny thing, windows shuttered . . ." the boy said, scratching his head. "Be that the one ye want?"

Connwood glanced at his companions. "Yes, I do think so."

"What are ye stopping fer, Jack?" the short, round man complained.

"Be ye no more than a twiddle-poop, ye snirp?" Jack returned. "We don't get our next purse till we meet wit that flash covey and show 'im we got the boy!"

"Be he coming 'ere?"

"Aye. Now stubble it, fer Gawd's sake," Jack returned in some disgust.

"Look 'ere, Jack, that be no way to talk to me. Oi be that hipped over this bobbery. Don't 'old wit chivying fancy morts! That will be yer rig when time comes—"

"Sh, 'ere comes flash now."

Lady Bee listened to all this and attempted to give Thomas an encouraging smile, until they both heard the next voice, all too familiar,

"Well, gentlemen," Felix Holland said, "have you done your job?"

"Aye, and then some," Jack said. "Ye didn't tell us about the fancy mort."

"What? A woman? What woman?" Felix's brow was up, and there was an anxious note in his voice.

"Came along wit the boy. It'll cost ye a pretty gold one more to do 'er in as well," Jack returned.

Felix went to the shutter and opened it, to find both Lady Barbara and Sir Thomas staring directly at him. He groaned and reshut the enclosure sharply. "Hell and brimstone!"

"That is Felix," Thomas said to Lady Bee inside the carriage. "Never liked him, even though he took me to the balloon ascension. But . . . why does he want to kill me?"

"I am afraid that desperate men are slaves to their own greed. It is not you he wants to kill; it is the object that stands between him and the money he would inherit if that object were removed. He doesn't think of you as a person . . . do you see?"

"Yes . . . I guess so." Thomas thought about this and then said, "What are we going to do?"

Barbara bit her bottom lip, for she didn't have an answer ready. She had hoped to play it by ear, but thus far, nothing had come along to aid her in this, and then they heard another familiar voice.

"Well, well, m'lads . . . Mr. Holland," said Mr. Tibbs in way of greeting.

"What in the name of . . . ?" Holland thundered. "Where did you spring from?" He was already slowly moving his hand inside his coat.

"Now, I wouldn't do that, Mr. Holland," Tibbs

said, leveling his gun at Felix Holland in a most menacing manner.

"No, of course not," Holland said, dropping his hand. "How the deuce did you come across this, and who the hell are you?"

"Well, and you know m'name. Tibbs. Bow Street runner ... hired by Mr. Russell at Lord Connwood's instigation, to watch over Sir Thomas 'ere." He inclined his head, "Me and his lordship, we go back a long way."

"May ye rot, runner!" hollered Jack Wold, who had managed to aim his gun and shoot.

He caught Mr. Tibbs in the shoulder, but it was enough to change the situation around, for Felix then went for the runner and had him in hand. "Over there—by the coach!" He looked around. This was a secluded alley, but was it secluded enough? Had anyone heard the shot? Felix wondered as he racked his brain for a solution to this new problem.

Connwood and his companions came to an intersection. They sat their fidgeting horses for a long moment as his lordship tried to decide which direction to take. Ahead of him the road narrowed, and the bustle of traffic seemed to dwindle.

"Come on," he said, leading them down the quiet avenue. They hadn't traveled very far when the sound of a shot came to their ears, and they exchanged glances. Connwood felt a certain fear grip his heart. Bee, his Bee, his love ... ? Silently they rushed toward the sound, and both his lordship and Fleetwood had their guns already in hand.

Jack Wold, his companion, and Felix Holland looked up at the sound of horses' hooves on pavement. "Damnation!" Holland breathed.

"We be getting out of 'ere," Jack announced, picking up the reins.

"Robby, block that side avenue," Connwood called as he spotted the coach down the road.

"Here!" Fleetwood called, throwing Robby his gun.

Robby caught it and cut diagonally across the road to block the coach's only means of escape, while Connwood and Fleetwood approached it head-on.

During the commotion Bee had applied herself to pushing on the shutter of her window. All at once it swung open.

"Thomas—here, let me help you into position and you push on the glass with your boots. That's my buck!"

The glass, when it fell, did so with a clatter and took Jack Wold's attention long enough for Mr. Tibbs to retrieve the gun he had dropped to the ground. He swung around and aimed it at Mr. Wold's companion, who was nearest to him. "Up with those ugly fambles of yours, my friend," Mr. Tibbs said.

Connwood didn't waste time speaking. He didn't waste time shouting out a warning. He leveled his gun at Mr. Wold, who had turned once more and aimed his gun at the riders coming toward him. With Connwood's single shot Mr. Wold was disarmed.

Felix had been watching all this, his own gun held with uncertainty. He was ruined. He was in debt, and now he would be labeled forever, in prison forever—he hadn't enough cash even to flee the country. He brought up his gun and aimed it at Connwood, who was attempting to reload.

Robby had closed at this point and saw at once that his lordship was in danger. He called for his friend's attention, "John!" There was no time. He had to make a split second decision, and it was to save his friend at Felix Holland's cost.

Connwood looked up at Robby, and their eyes met a moment before his lordship jumped off his horse and ran to the carriage. In some impatience he undid the roping that held the door secured. Lady Bee flung herself into his arms and nearly sent them both reeling backward. He caught her and they laughed in a moment of unbridled relief. He found himself kissing the top of her tawny head and stroking her, and then Bee released a sudden sob.

"Oh, my love, my only love, it's over, it's over." Connwood soothed.

Thomas jumped out of the coach and touched Bee's back. "She is a right un, my lord ... but I guess all girls like to cry."

Bee laughed and turned around to hug him to her. Then she looked up at his lordship and softly inquired, "Your love? Your only love?"

He kissed her forehead and then dropped a light kiss upon her cherry lips. "Wondrously so." And then he sighed as he realized the mess of a scandal they had on their hands. He had to get Lady Bee away from this ugly scene.

There was Felix Holland dead in the street in broad daylight! Connwood took Bee's hand and moved toward the Bow Street runner, who, in spite of his wound, was managing very well.

"Are you badly hurt, Tibbs?" His lordship surveyed his old friend.

"No more than usual. I'll do. The bullet went clean through."

"Yes, but it needs attention," his lordship cautioned.

"And so it will get when we get these brutes off the street," Tibbs returned.

"Right, then, I am going to get Lady Bee to her home. I shall leave you Mr. Huxley and Sir George."

"Aye, they'll do."

He turned to Bee. "Come on, then, You'll take Robby's horse. I want to get you home first. Thomas can ride double with me."

"Yes, but what about Robby?" Bee objected.

"Never mind Robby!" his lordship snapped, anxious now to have her well away from this scene. "He will be driving with Mr. Tibbs on the coach. Fleetwood will ride guard. Are you satisfied?"

Bee had, however, come round and had a full view of Holland lying still on the ground, and she gasped. She knew already that he was dead, but the sight of his body caused her to swerve in her purpose. His lordship saw this at once and took up her elbow, steering her away. "Come on then, little one, up on your mount," he said, giving her a leg up and taking the reins to lead her to his own horse, which had wandered off down the avenue.

Some moments later they made their way through Soho once more, and as Lady Bee watched his lordship manage the traffic of people, wagons, and horses, she felt a sure sadness. He had called her his love, his only love. What did that mean? What could it mean? Would he still go ahead and ask Lady Sarah to be his wife?

Chapter Twenty-Six

"Wait . . . wait . . . slow down," Bee's father commanded as his daughter attempted to recount the events of the day. "How did Mr. Tibbs appear? How did he know where to find you and Thomas?"

"As it happens," Robby answered, "he told Fleetwood and me that he realized that Thomas had slipped out of the house and if it hadn't been for his catching sight of our Bee here, he would have completely lost the lad. As it was, he only just managed to keep up when those ugly screws took to coach."

"Yes, but, Bee"—the earl was still astounded by all of this—"whatever made you take after Thomas like that?"

"Woman's intuition." She frowned and looked at Donna. "I rather thought that his lordship would have stopped by tonight to see how we are."

"Never mind, Bee," Donna said. "Things in that area are still pretty complicated, you know. There is still the Lady Sarah."

"Yes, I know, but I think she is in love with her Dennis Maxwell."

"I know, but I inquired. Her parents won't countenance the match. They are holding out for Connwood's offer."

"Oh, I see," Bee said in a small voice, and then added, "But, Donna, he called me his love, his only love."

"And so you are . . . but if he feels honor bound to offer for Lady Sarah, then even that can't change what must be." Donna saw her friend's expression and felt her own heart wrench. If only there were something she could do.

Bee had not been wrong. The Lady Sarah was certainly in love with her Dennis Maxwell, and she meant to have him. However, Donna was not wrong, either. Sarah's parents still expected an offer to come from Connwood and would not agree to the inferior match while his lordship's proposal was a distinct possibility. Sarah took matters into her own hands. She arrived at Connwood's bachelor lodgings and demanded admittance. This rather shocked Connwood's butler. However, he led her to the study and announced her to Connwood, who was attempting to soothe his agitated spirits by drinking himself into a stupor.

"Oh, no—never say you are in your cups, John?" Lady Sarah cried, going toward him.

"Not yet, but before the night is out, I intend to be. Why?"

"I need your help, and that means you must be coherent."

"You need my help?" He sighed and motioned for her to sit. He waited till she was comfortable and pulling off her gloves, then said idly, "You shouldn't be here, you know. Most improper. Your mama would not approve."

"I wore a veil over my face and took a hackney. No one observed me. Never mind that now." She looked at him steadily. "How do you feel about me, John?"

160

"What kind of a question is that?" He avoided answering directly.

"Never mind. You are too much a gentleman to be forthright with me, so I shall take this matter neatly in hand. We are not in love with each other. *I* am, in fact, very much in love with Mr. Maxwell, whom you know. However, my parents will not consent to a match between us while you are still available."

"What do you suggest?" Connwood's eyes had lit with hope.

"You cannot cry off and retain your honor, I understand that. However, if you were to catch me with Mr. Maxwell . . . you would have no choice but to waive your wishes in the matter, and my parents would have to avoid scandal by consenting to my marriage to Dennis."

Connwood grabbed her and smacked her lips with his own. "For the first time, my Lady Sarah, I almost love you!"

"Really? Well, I could almost feel insulted, but never mind, for we need to discuss how this will be done . . . and where."

"You have a plan formed in your amazing mind, I think," he answered happily.

"Indeed, I am permitted to attend Lady Barbara's ball, though I must not dance, and it is my intention that we handle our scheme at her ball."

"Is it?" he returned. "Indeed, I like your plan already."

"Donna, should I wear these pearls?" Bee asked, smoothing her hands over the white-and-silver ball gown.

"For pity's sake, girl, of course. They match the little pearl drops in your ears and the threading of pearls in your hair. You look perfect—just perfect."

She eyed herself in the looking glass. "Do you think I should wear the topaz or the diamonds Robby gave me yesterday?"

"Stupid. The topaz set matches the silver so wondrously." Bee moved across her bedroom in some agitation, and Donna eyed her thoughtfully. "Bee . . . you know, you are very beautiful. You just shine."

"Beautiful enough to be happy?" Bee asked sadly.

"Idiot child." Donna laughed. "You will have every man at the ball at your feet."

"I only want Connwood," Bee answered sadly.

"Come on, you are going to be late for your own ball," Donna said, taking her hand and pulling her along.

It was nearly an hour later when Bee finally caught sight of Lord Connwood striding through the ballroom doors and toward her. Faith, but he took her breath away. His ginger-gray hair fell in silken waves around his handsome face, and his eyes caressed her as he approached.

"My Lady Barbara, you will break hearts tonight," he said softly. "My own included."

"Never yours," she answered just as softly.

He looked past her then and frowned. "You will excuse me a moment, for I see Lady Sarah. . . ."

Lady Bee felt her heart torn out of her chest at that. She watched him walk away and then nearly ran into Fleetwood's arms. He had witnessed the scene and held her by her shoulders.

"What's this?" he demanded. "Come and waltz with me."

"He didn't even ask me to," Bee said, looking up at her friend.

"More fool, he," Fleetwood said gently and led her onto the floor.

Donna watched all this and looked to Connwood

for her cue. He was leaving the ballroom now, turning to look at her and imperceptibly nodding in her direction. She excused herself from the earl, who had been wondering if she had heard a word he had said to her, and moved toward Lady Grey's set. She took a moment to brace herself, for Lady Sarah's mother was a formidable lady. However, she knew what she had to do,

"Lady Grey . . ." Donna said.

"Yes? Ah, you are Mrs. Huxley, aren't you? We met, I think, at Searington."

"Yes. I think you should come with me," Donna said.

"What? Why?" Her ladyship was surprised.

"Your daughter . . . needs you."

"What do you mean, my daughter needs me?" Lady Grey demanded.

Donna attempted to say more with her eyes and nearly glared at her ladyship. "Please, my lady, do come."

"Oh, very well, though this is very irregular," her ladyship said in some irritation.

"What is going on?" Bee asked Fleetwood.

"What do you mean?" Fleetwood returned, not meeting her gaze.

"You know something," Bee accused.

"Something? I should hope so," Fleetwood said, attempting to tease her away from her purpose.

"Fleetie!" Bee nearly stamped her foot.

"Mind your steps," he reproved.

"Yes, but . . . why has everybody left the ballroom?" she persisted.

"Dearest, are you well? Has your sight been giving you trouble? Seems to me, there is a sight more people in this ballroom than you would want."

"Fleetie! You know who I mean. First Connwood, after his Lady Sarah and her beau, then Donna and Lady Grey—what is going on?"

"Look—there is Beau Brummell smiling at you," Fleetwood said in answer to her question.

"Well, I shall find out," Bee said, pulling out of his hold and moving through the squeeze of people toward the double doors.

Fleetwood raised his eyes heavenward and then shrugged his shoulders; well, he thought, as he started to follow her, might as well join the tryst!

The "tryst," as it were, was in full swing within the cozy confines of the library, where Lady Sarah had led her love.

"Put your arms round me, Dennis," she demanded.

He eyed her doubtfully. "But, my darling—"

"Please don't be so tiresome. Quickly, now."

"Yes, but do you think that we should?"

"Dennis." The lady pouted. "Don't you want to put your arms round me?"

"With all my heart, dearest, but—"

She heard someone at the threshold of the library door and flung her arms round her beau in a heady fashion and ordered him in almost rough terms, "Kiss me, you fool!"

Dennis's brows went up, but there was no time to remonstrate with his beloved, for she then attached her lips to his own in noisy, lusty fashion.

"What have we here?" Lord Connwood inquired glibly.

Dennis had been told by his love what the plan was. He knew what to expect, and still he had a difficult time overcoming his embarrassment. He found himself coloring to the roots of his fair hair,

while his dear heart answered Connwood, "Mercy—
my lord." She remained fixed to her Dennis in a
most clinging fashion.

"Indeed, shall I take this to mean that I need not
apply to your father for your hand, as we had once
thought I should?"

"What in heaven's name is going on here?" cried
Lady Grey, who had arrived in time to find her
daughter hugging Dennis Maxwell to herself in a
most compromising position. She could see that
Connwood had discovered this treacherous piece of
business and was about to cry off. She turned to
Connwood and nearly pleaded, "My lord, I don't
know what is going on but—"

"What is going on is obvious, my lady. I would
never dream of standing in the way of Lady Sarah's
happiness, which is what I would be doing if I persisted in my original desire to apply for her hand
in marriage." He turned to Sarah and managed the
smallest of winks. "I trust that you shall not live
to regret this day's work."

"But, my lord," Lady Grey persisted, "you cannot—I mean, she is a child, she doesn't know what
she is doing. . . ."

"She is not a child and has displayed that very
well. Allow her to know her own mind." He suddenly felt something and knew that Bee was
nearby. He looked toward the doors and saw her
standing there, her pretty mouth wide open, and he
smiled. "As for me, I shall be making an announcement about my own future very soon . . . tonight,
in fact." He walked toward Bee, took up both her
hands and put them to his lips. To her he said, "After I speak with your father, will you do me the
honour of becoming my bride?"

Lady Bee squealed with delight, and as everyone

165

in the room had lost all sense of propriety anyway, decided she might as well do the same. She threw her arms round his lordship and showed him how very honored she meant to make him!

Dorothy Dowdell...

romantic novels of proud women who confront the perils of passion and adventure.